THE JEDERA
ADVENTURE

OTHER YEARLING BOOKS YOU WILL ENJOY:

YEARLING BOOKS/YOUNG YEARLINGS/YEARLING CLASSICS are designed especially to entertain and enlighten young people. Patricia Reilly Giff, consultant to this series, received the bachelor's degree from Marymount College. She holds the master's degree in history from St. John's University, and a Professional Diploma in Reading from Hofstra University. She was a teacher and reading consultant for many years, and is the author of numerous books for young readers.

For a complete listing of all Yearling titles,
write to Dell Readers Service,
P.O. Box 1045, South Holland, IL 60473.

THE JEDERA
ADVENTURE

❧ ❧

LLOYD ALEXANDER

A Yearling Book

Published by
Dell Publishing
a division of
Bantam Doubleday Dell Publishing Group, Inc.
666 Fifth Avenue
New York, New York 10103

ISBN: 0-440-40295-6

Reprinted by arrangement with E.P. Dutton, a division of Penguin
Books USA Inc.

Printed in the United States of America

May 1990

10 9 8 7 6 5 4 3 2 1

OPM

for all fond traveling companions

THE JEDERA
ADVENTURE

Map by Debby L. Carter

1

Miss Vesper Holly believes in keeping promises. Sometimes I wish she did not.

"Brinnie, what if somebody borrows a book and forgets to give it back?"

When Vesper asks one question, she usually has a few others in mind. But I had spent all a spring afternoon in 1874 floundering through a swamp of mildewed travel notes, and I welcomed the interruption.

"Dear girl, it must be returned, no matter what the circumstances. It is a sacred obligation."

"I think so, too," said Vesper. "What happened is, I came across this library book and—well, it's overdue."

"Better late than never," I said. "Overdue? How long?"

"A while," said Vesper. "Fifteen years."

"But—but that is unconscionable! Inexcusable, beyond explanation!"

"Father borrowed it."

That was explanation enough. The late Dr. Benjamin

Rittenhouse Holly, my old friend and traveling companion, a brilliant scholar, a fearless adventurer, tended to ignore trivial details. This included overdue library books.

Vesper now produced the object in question. It was a treatise on the curative powers of medicinal herbs, an exquisite little volume handwritten on vellum in ancient Arabic calligraphy. Its age might be eight hundred years; its value, incalculable.

"Do you realize who wrote this?" I could hardly believe my eyes. "The greatest physician of his day. Ibn-Sina—'Avicenna,' as we call him. A work from his own hand. Priceless!"

"Beautiful." Vesper carefully turned the pages, their margins filled with brightly colored, interlaced patterns. "A real treasure. But I don't suppose we should keep it."

"Certainly not. That would be dishonorable, worse than thievery. As your father's executor," I said, "I take the responsibility for returning it. I shall do so immediately."

"I hoped you would," said Vesper.

"You have my word," I assured her, and went on to suggest that a mere letter of apology would hardly suffice. Embarrassing though it might be after fifteen years of tardiness, I proposed handing such a valuable item personally to the director.

"I should be there, too," said Vesper.

"So you shall. That would be only fitting and proper. We must do so without further delay. Perhaps this very afternoon. The volume no doubt came from some special collection at the Library Company of Philadelphia or the University of Pennsylvania."

"Not exactly."

"Where, then?" I could think of no other institutions apart from Philadelphia's that could boast of possessing such a bibliographic gem. Surely not Harvard.

"Bel-Saaba," said Vesper.

I nearly sprang out of my chair and my skin. "Good heavens, you cannot mean—"

"The Bel-Saaba library," said Vesper. "In Jedera. You must know about it."

What scholar did not? For centuries, the city of Bel-Saaba had been one of North Africa's commercial and cultural centers. Its library was world renowned, a repository for every kind of lore and learning, of ancient texts on mathematics, medicine, astronomy, physics.

Indeed, I knew of Bel-Saaba. But why, I asked, did Vesper suppose the book had come from there?

"I found this between the pages."

She handed me a small sheet of parchment. With her astonishing gift for languages, Vesper is more fluent in Arabic than I am, but I could follow the brief text easily enough. It was a copy of a receipt, dated 1859, specifying the volume's origin and promising—under all manner of solemn vows—to return it; the signature, unmistakably Holly's.

"As you said, Brinnie, it's a sacred obligation. No way around it, we have to go."

I reminded her that Bel-Saaba, at the southernmost border of Jedera, lay beyond a notoriously rugged mountain range and across a disagreeable stretch of desert.

"It is a bit out of the way," admitted Vesper, "but I don't see any other choice."

"The postal service?" It was a feeble suggestion, but the best I could muster. "If we mailed it? Carefully wrapped."

"I doubt that there's local delivery," replied Vesper. "And you did say it should be handed over personally. It can't be all that hard. There must be trade routes. Caravan trails. Plenty of camels."

"Too many." I have had some experience with camels. For contrariness and foul temper, and a disgusting habit of expectorating, the creature is surpassed only by a Philadelphia banker.

Vesper shrugged. For a girl of eighteen, she can assume an air of bland innocence that a riverboat gambler, a rug merchant, or a horse trader would spend a lifetime perfecting.

"Whatever you think best. Still, you did give your word."

"Dear girl," I protested, "that was before I had any notion—"

"It's all right. I understand. A person can't always keep a promise. Not even my dear old Brinnie."

Vesper can be utterly diabolical when she chooses. But at that moment a rescuing angel came into the library: my wife, Mary, summoning us to tea.

I turned to her in joyous hope. Mary had taken over the smooth running of the household a few years previously, when Vesper moved us lock, stock, and barrel—including my beehives and unfinished history of the Etruscans—into her Strafford mansion. Mary and I, Professor Brinton Garrett, were Vesper's guardians. Mary would agree that we could not permit her to undertake the hardship, even danger, of such an enterprise. I quickly explained the circumstances.

Mary frowned and shook her head. "I do not approve of this kind of journey merely for the sake of a book by Ibn-what's-his-name."

I breathed a sigh of relief.

"However," Mary went on, "though I wish you had not, you did make a promise."

"Dear Mary," I exclaimed, "are you, of all people, saying Vesper and I should go camel riding into a howling desert?"

"No. I am only saying, dear Brinnie, that you and I have always believed it our solemn duty to keep promises."

Vesper had already embroiled me in earthquakes, rebellions, and attacks by ferocious hounds; she had saved my life on numerous occasions—after causing me to risk it in the first place. Now she proposed a foolhardy errand in some camel-infested corner of the world.

"When do we start?" I said.

CHAPTER

2

Vesper, needless to say, lost no time embarking for Jedera. After a fairly smooth and rapid crossing, we docked in the capital, Mokarra, pink-walled under the granite shadow of Jebel Kasar, and began making the rounds of shipping offices and tourist agencies. My thought was to attach ourselves, for comfort and safety, to a large trading caravan led by an experienced guide.

We first encountered a hard-bitten cameleer in a battered crimson fez. Before Vesper could begin explaining our purpose, he assured us we had luckily come to the right place.

"Here you see the finest guide in all Jedera," he declared. "The prince—no, the king of caravans. I plead for the honor of serving you."

He did, in fact, look willing to transport his grandmother to the moon if the price was right.

"Yes, well," said Vesper, "we want to go—"

"It makes no difference," he broke in. "Wherever you choose, beautiful *anisah*. We can depart this instant for any corner of the world." He laid his hands on his chest and bowed. "I stand ready. My camels paw the ground in impatience. Only name your destination."

"We'd like to go to Bel-Saaba," said Vesper.

He abruptly straightened.

"Shall I waste my time with fools and maniacs?" He waved his arms at us. "Go! Out! Out! You have no dealings with me." He turned away, muttering something uncomplimentary about crazy *roumis,* as the Jederans termed any foreigners.

"I don't think he's much interested," observed Vesper.

We continued on our rounds, meeting with similar reactions, and I began to wonder if this was one library book that would be permanently overdue. At last, we did turn up a caravan leader willing to let us join him. He was expecting a freighter to arrive with a cargo of goods for transport direct to Bel-Saaba.

Vesper, delighted, asked when the ship was due in port. The caravan leader shrugged. He could not be certain. Perhaps within the next two days. Or three. Or four. Who could speak for the winds and tides?

With this, we had to be content. But now, at least assured of transportation, Vesper wished to turn the delay to advantage by sightseeing. We had found accommodations in a *serai,* a sort of inn, or public lodging house, and quite excellent they were: airy chambers, with our own private courtyard and surrounding garden, a sparkling little fountain, a pomegranate tree.

From this quiet haven, we set off across the public square. Vesper has a taste for commotion, and it was more than satisfied. For myself, I expected to go deaf at any moment. In addition to vendors hawking spicy kabobs, candied rose leaves, and steaming pilaf, drummers pounded away, flute players shrilled, street singers gargled and warbled, and everyone else seemed to be shouting and haggling at the top of their voices. Vesper loved it.

"Brinnie, what's over there?"

She led me into a loose ring of onlookers. What had caught her eye seemed to be a heap of whirling rags—until I realized it had arms and legs, and feet where its head should have been.

Dancing on his hands, spinning like a top, turning somersaults in mid-air, this street performer held Vesper's fascinated attention. She laughed gleefully and tossed down some coins, which he somehow snatched up with his flexible, and grimy, toes. Then, quitting his acrobatics, he squatted cross-legged, popped the coins into his mouth, and an instant later produced them from his nose.

"I want to learn that trick," said Vesper.

But now the fellow began a different performance: borrowing small objects from his audience and tossing them into the air, where they suddenly vanished only to reappear from unlikely areas of his anatomy.

We observed his antics for a while. Vesper, I thought, could spend her time in ways more uplifting than watching a vagabond's sleight of hand. I drew her aside, suggesting a tour of the French colonial administration buildings. Vesper reluctantly started to follow me. A moment later, she halted and turned back at the sound of bloodcurdling yells.

CHAPTER

3

Two of the onlookers had seized the fellow by his legs and were vigorously bouncing him up and down. Despite his yelping and struggling, the pair kept on as if determined to take him apart piece by piece.

"That's not part of the act," said Vesper.

She pushed through the knot of bystanders. By now, the vagabond was in danger of a serious beating, for a couple more members of his audience had joined in.

"Let him up!" Vesper cried. "Are you trying to kill him?"

That appeared to be their goal. They might have had good reason, but Vesper did not wait for any explanation. She collared one of the assailants and flung him aside. The other, startled by her unexpected onslaught, loosened his grip. The vagabond collapsed in a heap.

Vesper has a forceful personality in any circumstances. In addition, the sudden arrival of a green-eyed, marmalade-haired *roumi,* impeccably garbed in elegant travel costume, left the audience dumbstruck for a few seconds, after which, they began shouting at her all at once, shaking their fists at the performer and making other gestures of disapproval.

The best I could gather from their racket was that "Maleesh," as they called him, was the thieving offspring of a diseased camel. He had borrowed a ring from one of the bystanders, caused it to vanish—but neglected to make it reappear.

The object of this accusation had meanwhile climbed to his feet. If the Jederans employed scarecrows, he would have qualified as a distinguished member of that profession. He appeared to be young, hardly past his middle twenties. Thus, it was all the more remarkable that he should have become so bedraggled in so few years. Yet, as he addressed Vesper, he did manage to convey a certain tattered dignity.

"That is a lie, *anisah,*" Maleesh declared. "The veritable grandfather of lies. My fingers slipped. The ring fell. I lost it."

Some disagreement followed his protest, and I feared they would start belaboring him again. However, in every corner of the world, the offer of cash has a soothing effect. Vesper, from her purse, gave handsome amounts to the plaintiff and his witnesses. It amounted to straightforward bribery and was immediately effective. The bystanders drifted away.

All but one. A tall, hooded figure cloaked in a burnoose lingered a moment. Perhaps it was my imagination, but he seemed about to approach us. Then, as if thinking better of it, he turned aside and strode into the crowd.

Maleesh, meantime, had thrown himself at Vesper's feet and flung his arms around her ankles.

"*Anisah*, you have saved my life! Daughter of the sun and moon! Oasis of my dismal existence! Angel from the seventh paradise!"

"I wouldn't go all that far," said Vesper.

We were not in the situation or posture for a formal introduction. Vesper, nevertheless, made one. Maleesh transferred his embrace from her ankles to mine.

"Bahrini el-Garra!" he cried, attempting to pronounce my name. "My gratitude, *sidi*, is eternal!"

The fellow was a barnacle with legs. The only thing that made him release his grip on me was Vesper presenting him with a handful of coins.

"May the heavens guide your footsteps," exclaimed Maleesh. "I call down the smile of the universe upon you."

Feeling this was ample thanks, I turned away and drew Vesper along with me. I was proud of her generous, compassionate conduct befitting a true daughter of Philadelphia and treated her to a glass of mint tea.

As we relaxed on the terrace of a refreshment shop, I could have sworn the burnoose-clad figure loitered nearby. I gave it no further thought, for the racket in the square had begun making my head ache, muddling any serious speculation. When Vesper suggested visiting the casbah, I welcomed the chance. This most ancient part of Mokarra supposedly contained the thieves' quarter. Thievery being a stealthy occupation, I hoped the casbah would at least be quiet.

It was not. Troops of urchins raced yelling and whooping through the maze of narrow streets and winding flights of stone steps. Women laughed and gossiped from doorways or open windows. In the local *souk*, or open-air market, hucksters tried to outdo each other in praising their fruits and vegetables.

There was much to capture our attention, but Vesper must have eyes in the back of her head.

"Brinnie," she murmured, "we're being followed."

I had not noticed. But now I turned to glance back, half expecting to see the man in the burnoose. Instead, I glimpsed Maleesh, stalking along some paces behind us.

"He's been on our heels for at least ten minutes."

The fellow was not only a barnacle, he was a leech. Clearly, he saw Vesper as a source of further wealth. I turned on my heel and went to confront him.

"My good sir," I said firmly, "this kind lady has already saved your life. She has also given you money, which you may or may not have deserved. Be satisfied. Charity has its limits."

"I am not a beggar, Sidi Bahrini," replied Maleesh, drawing himself erect. "Have I asked for alms?"

Vesper had come to join me. Maleesh turned to her.

"*Anisah,* you have done all good things for me. You have bound my destiny to yours with a golden chain."

If that were so, I told him, I suggested unlinking the connection and requested him to cease following us.

"I cannot do that. Our fates are joined. So it is written."

He made this pronouncement with such solemn intensity that Vesper could not help grinning at him.

"I don't remember reading that anywhere, Maleesh. Where is it written?"

"Why, *anisah,* it is written in the stars." He gestured upward in the direction of those celestial bodies, though

14

he seemed, instead, to be pointing at a clothesline of multicolored laundry slung between opposite windows.

"I am your servant, your slave," he declared. "So it must be. I am yours to command."

His services, I replied, were not required. Our command was for him to depart. We wished to see no more of him.

"I am still your slave," answered Maleesh. "If my presence burdens you, then I obey your wishes. So be it."

"No—wait a minute," Vesper put in.

By then, however, Maleesh had disappeared around the corner. Vesper hurried after him, but the vagabond must have nipped into one of the alleys and lost himself in the shadows. He had taken my command literally.

"I wanted to ask him how he did that coin trick," said Vesper.

She insisted on searching the adjoining streets, but we saw not a trace of him.

We returned to our lodgings after that. Next morning, we went to the square. Vesper had two objectives: one, to seek news of the vessel carrying cargo for Bel-Saaba; the other, to find Maleesh.

What we found was a disaster.

No sooner had we started for the waterfront than we were caught up in a stream of Mokarrans shouting and racing toward the harbor. Clouds of evil-smelling smoke were rising from the port.

We could not help ourselves, we were borne along in the crowd, pressed and jostled to the dockside. A freighter had caught fire and was blazing out of control.

The vessels moored nearby were hurriedly casting

loose. A couple of feluccas, equipped with oars as well as sail, were rowing seaward; a trim, ocean-going yacht had already given a wide berth to the flaming ship.

The fire must have broken out in the midst of off-loading the cargo. Longshoremen frantically rolled barrels as far out of danger as possible or heaved those beginning to burn into the water, the ship's crew lending a hand. Over all hung a peculiar, stifling reek.

"Kerosene?" Vesper wrinkled her nose.

I had no chance to comment. The onlookers swept her away from me. For a moment, I lost sight of her and forced my way through the crowd, calling her name.

Finally, near the landing stage, I caught a glimpse of her and cried out in alarm. Vesper was struggling in the clutches of two burly sailors.

CHAPTER

4

"Brinnie, come on! Hurry!"

Vesper had sighted me; the dear girl's voice rang bravely above the tumult. Shouting encouragement, urging her not to despair, I fought through the crowd, heaving aside the curiosity seekers blocking my way, to fling myself on one of the sailors. I gripped the ruffian in the ninja death lock. The effect would have been devastating had the wretch's neck not been so short and his shoulders so heavily muscled. He grunted in surprise at the ferocity of my attack but shrugged himself loose.

Vesper has always been able to give a good account of herself, even against such powerful odds. Now, to my bewilderment, she was making no attempt at defense or any effort to escape the sailors' clutches. On the contrary, she actually seemed to be trying her best to embrace both of them at the same time.

I had stretched out my arms to renew my assault, only to find my hands caught and pumped up and down, one by each sailor.

"Look who's here," cried Vesper.

I blinked in disbelief at their smoke-blackened features, unable for the life of me to tell one from the other. Their moon-round faces, fringes of grizzled hair, and freckled domes were identical.

"Smiler and Slider." Vesper beamed at them. "Here, of all places, can you imagine?"

I could not. We had last seen the twins—how many thousand miles away?—in El Dorado, working Blazer O'Hara's riverboat. I was doubly astonished. Literally.

"Miss Vesper has it right." Smiler—or Slider—finally released my hand, and his brother did likewise. "Here, of all places."

"And here we'll have to stay," added Slider—or Smiler. "We're aground, sir. Beached, in a manner of speaking."

"Burnt out is the fact of it," added Slider.

"That's their ship," said Vesper. "Or, it used to be."

Our attention had been so caught up by this happy, though startling, reunion with the twins that I had momentarily forgotten the flaming vessel. By this time, there was little of it to remember. Although the crew, I gathered, had escaped unharmed, the freighter had burned to the waterline. Smiler and Slider shaded their pale blue eyes, both gazing with equal dismay at the charred hulk.

"*Our* ship, too," said Vesper. "The one we've been waiting for. The cargo—those barrels are going to Bel-Saaba."

"What's left of them," said Smiler. "That's correct, sir, as I told Miss Vesper. As for when they'll go, there's no guessing. By the time they're inspected and inventoried

18

and claimed for insurance— Slider knows more of the ins and outs of such business than I do."

"Yes, and the captain is likely to be charged with endangering the port," said Slider. "Not to mention all the foreign red tape, a kind you don't find in the States. So, it can stretch out a good long while."

"We'll get along though," said Smiler. "It's times like this when we're all the more grateful to be twins. We keep each other the best of company, and that's a consolation when you're lost in a distant clime."

"You aren't lost," said Vesper. "You're found. First thing, you'll come with us."

Vesper led the twins from the stench and smoke of the port to the calm of the little courtyard. We sat comfortably by the fountain while Vesper asked for news of El Dorado and why Smiler and Slider had left that Central American republic. "Nothing wrong, is there?"

"Far from it," said Smiler. "We're all thriving and prospering. That's the only trouble."

"Old Blazer's retired," Slider added, "and so's the *Libertador*; the boat's past repair. But that Frenchy, de Rochefort—changed his name from Alain to Allano, he's that fond of the Chirican Indians—he fixed up that villain Helvitius's yacht for the river trade. Thanks to you, miss, things have never been better for the tribe. And for him, since he and Suncha tied the wedding knot."

"Slider and I trained a crew of Chiricans for engineers and pilots," continued Smiler. "They turned out better than us. What it came down to was, we hadn't much to do. It's restless-making. So, to occupy our time, as you might say, we took a berth on that freighter."

"And here we are, as you see us," said Slider.

"And Acharro?" asked Vesper. "He's well? He's still chief?"

"Every bit of one," replied Smiler. "He talks of you a lot, Miss Vesper. I'd go so far as to say—"

"Yes, well," broke in Vesper, as her cheeks flushed a little—or perhaps it was the afternoon light, "I think of him, too. But what I'm thinking right now is that we couldn't have run into you at a better time."

She explained our reason for coming to Jedera and her determination to reach Bel-Saaba. "If you'd like to go there with us—"

Here, I reminded her that it could be a long while before we went anywhere. The caravan would be indefinitely, even permanently, delayed.

"That's why I'm glad we ran into you. Why wait to join a caravan? We could have our own.

"If the twins agree," she added, "that's four of us. Safe enough to suit you, Brinnie. And I can certainly read a map."

Anxious though I was to finish my noble duty, to me the scheme was impractical. Vesper, I admitted, could make her way through any ordinary howling wilderness. But the Haggar Mountains, let alone the desert crossing, would be too much even for her remarkable abilities. Furthermore, assembling the necessary pack animals, provisions, tents, and other equipment would present a formidable task.

"That's where you come in," she replied. "Dear old Brinnie, you know you're a genius at organizing things. You'll find all we need in the bazaar. Camels, too, I'd suppose."

Purchasing camels, I protested, was a highly special-
ized skill. In any case, the twins had not been given the
opportunity to express their own views.

"If I can speak for Slider—" Smiler began.

"As you certainly can," put in Slider, clasping his twin
warmly by the hand. "We're always of the same mind.
Yes, we'll be glad to oblige. We've never had any dealings with camels, outside a zoo, but they can't be crankier
than the old *Libertador.*"

" 'Ships of the desert,' as they're called," said Smiler,
"and ships is what we know. Square-rigged or four-
legged, it should be one and the same."

"Settled, then," declared Vesper. "Brinnie can start to-
morrow."

The twins had ceased paying attention. They suddenly
leaned their heads together and exchanged a few whispered words.

As Vesper watched, puzzled, the twins stood and
stretched, announcing that they felt the simultaneous need
to retire to their sleeping quarters.

Slider strolled off in one direction, Smiler in another.
The day's happenings had, I feared, been too much of a
strain on their minds. Their decision to go along with Vesper's proposal would have been proof enough that they
had temporarily taken leave of their senses. I was all the
more convinced when they started racing from opposite
directions to meet at the pomegranate tree and begin furiously shaking it.

What tumbled out was not a pomegranate.

CHAPTER

❧ 5 ❧

Vesper jumped to her feet. "Maleesh!"

The twins, meantime, had laid hold of the vagabond and hauled him before us.

"Do you know him, miss?" said Smiler. "We're sorry. We thought it was an intruder."

"It is," I remarked.

"I have only obeyed Sidi Bahrini's command," said Maleesh, with more aplomb than might be expected from someone who had just been shaken out of a tree. "I did not wish to trouble you with my presence. It is not my fault that these twin moons of the heavens turned their gaze on the pomegranates of my hiding place. But they did well. For now I can do you a service: to warn you that your plan is ill-starred. The worst misfortunes will come from it. So it is written, and so it is."

"So it has been eavesdropped on," I said.

"Let him tell us what he means," Vesper said. "Misfortunes? Why? What's wrong with our plan?"

"First, do not assemble your caravan here," said Maleesh. "Why travel heavy-laden at the start? No, you should go lightly and easily to the gateway of the Haggar, Tizi Bekir. There, you shall buy all you need for the rest of the journey."

Vesper pondered for a moment. "That makes good sense. It's a fine suggestion, Maleesh. Thank you."

"But then, *anisah,* most important: Do not cross the Haggar and the Sahkra desert without a guide. You must have one who knows the turnings and twistings of the trail, who can speak the language of your camels, and who will guard you with his life."

"You're right." Vesper smiled. "You wouldn't, by luck, know such a guide?"

"Not by luck, by destiny," Maleesh corrected. "It is myself. I was born in the Haggar. I know every stone, every grain of desert sand. Did I not tell you our fortunes are linked? I shall be your guide and protector."

Being led through rough country by a street magician whose only demonstrated abilities were dancing on his hands and pulling coins from his nose did not inspire confidence. Vesper, however, had been studying Maleesh with that penetrating glance of hers. Finally, she nodded.

"If you really know the way—all right, we'll give you a try. But," she went on, as Maleesh seemed ready to fling himself around her ankles, "we'll take one step at a time. First, go with Brinnie and buy what we need for a start. We'll see about the rest in Tizi Bekir."

"Lo, it is written in the stars!" cried Maleesh.

I preferred it to be written in soap and water. Before anything else, Maleesh would have to take a bath.

I would be less than honest if I did not admit to occasions when my judgment might have been overhasty and when Vesper's insight proved clearer than my own. Maleesh was such an example. By the time he finished soaking and scrubbing himself, and exchanged his rags for some of my spare garments, he actually attained a modest level of respectability.

If this were not miracle enough, I must give him further credit. In choosing horses for us to ride and pack mules to carry our baggage, as we would not yet need camels, he showed himself to be an excellent, hardheaded bargainer. Since our present supply of clothing would serve us for the time being, he purchased only some burnooses, and those long, hooded robes proved to be as comfortable and practical as any garment in the world.

Thus, leaving the next morning to head south for Tizi Bekir, we indeed traveled lightly and quickly. We passed through a wide countryside of orchards and vineyards and soon came into a sparse, gritty landscape with only the rare stretch of greenery.

Vesper was thoroughly delighted by the efficiency of our little caravan. In this regard, Maleesh further astonished me. From the outset, he took charge of every detail. He chose the most suitable places to halt and organized our campsite, rationed out the water, built cook fires, served our food, and stood watch over us while we slept.

Though Smiler and Slider were not lacking in Yankee ingenuity, Maleesh taught them any number of special tricks in packing and unpacking our supplies, harnessing our animals, and giving the Jederan equivalents of *giddyup* and *whoa.* The twins willingly accepted his authority in such matters and quite happily and comfortably put themselves under his orders.

"We've done our share of traveling," said Smiler, with heartfelt admiration, "but we haven't met a fellow better at his job than Mr. Maleesh. We're glad to have him aboard."

For sailors, the twins proved unexpectedly skillful at riding and handling their mounts, which made Vesper wonder about their previous occupations.

"Why, we've turned our hand to all manner of things," replied Slider in answer to her inquiry on that subject. "Horses, among others."

"And would still be doing so," put in Smiler, "if there hadn't been that unhappy misunderstanding. A judicial disagreement, as you might say. We haven't been in the States since then."

"We get a touch homesick now and again," said Slider, "but we always cheer each other up. That's the blessing of being twins."

Otherwise, the pair chose to remain vague about their previous employments. Maleesh had equally little to say about his own past.

"My village is Ait-Kelah, deep in the Haggar," Maleesh told her. "My tribe, the Beni-Hareet."

"Why didn't you stay?" Vesper asked.

Maleesh ruefully shook his head. "I believed, *anisah*, that my fortune lay not in some narrow village but a great city. And so I went to Mokarra. Woe unto me! I found no fortune, only the scrapings of a bare living, small tricks for even smaller pittances." Then he brightened. "Until now. Lo, *anisah*, it is written. You and I shall prosper together."

25

"I hope you're right," said Vesper. She pressed him for no further details—except instruction in his coin trick. She and Maleesh practiced at every halt, and she quickly grew adept. What a Philadelphian might have thought of her squatting in the dust, producing coins from her nose, I did not wish to imagine. Fortunately, we met none along the way.

Tizi Bekir—the town bore the same name as the mountain pass—must have been more than a thousand years old. And looked it. The black, jagged heights of the Haggar rose abruptly behind it, but the town itself was as flat as a pancake and considerably drier. It had a jostling, lawless atmosphere not unlike some of our notorious Western frontier settlements, only without the presence of a sheriff to keep order.

Here, Maleesh told us, we would buy the camels we needed. For riding as well as carrying our equipment, he assured us the creatures would be reliable on the most difficult mountain trails as well as in the desert.

Maleesh picked out lodgings in what he judged to be the best *serai*, and he and the twins set about unpacking our gear. Vesper was impatient to see what livestock was available, and so, while Maleesh arranged our temporary living quarters, she and I went off on our own.

"Maleesh will find us when he's done," said Vesper. "We can have a little look around in the meantime."

There was no shortage of camel dealers. At the first place we stopped, however, the animals were clearly in poor condition. We pressed on through the crowd. Vesper halted at a line of ill-tempered beasts tethered in the shade of a canvas awning.

"These look better than the others, certainly," Vesper

said, nimbly avoiding being nipped or kicked. "But—Brinnie, I just don't know. Maleesh is the expert. We'd better wait for him. He can tell if they're fit to carry us to Bel-Saaba."

Just then, from the tail of my eye, I glimpsed what seemed a tall figure I had seen before: the hooded man in Mokarra. This time it was surely not my imagination. Before I could mention this peculiar coincidence to Vesper, the camel trader sidled up to us.

"You are going to Bel-Saaba?"

The proprietor was a heavyset, sharp-eyed fellow with a red fez cocked on the side of his gleaming bald head. Naming himself as Bou-Makari, he took us by the arm and addressed us in low, confidential tones.

"Have my ears deceived me? Truly, is it your intention to go on such a journey? Do you understand the difficulty of your enterprise?"

The first difficulty of our enterprise, I replied, was finding reliable transportation. As Philadelphians, we had little experience in evaluating camels.

"So distant from your home and you choose to go still farther?" Bou-Makari shook his head in wonder and admiration. "You are courageous, you and the lovely *anisah.* The Haggar, the Sahkra, can swallow up lone travelers without a trace."

"We'll manage," said Vesper. "Now, about these camels—"

"Worthless!" Bou-Makari snorted and waved a scornful hand. "It is not in my heart to deceive you. They will not serve your purpose. No, no, even if you begged me, I would not sell you such inferior merchandise.

"I have better stock," he went on, motioning for us to

follow him. "Of such excellence I do not offer them to any common buyers—*pfah,* what do they know of quality! Only for your sake, *anisah,* would I part with a few."

He went rattling on, praising his livestock, declaring that he treasured them as his own children, all the while leading us around the corner and a little way from the bazaar.

"Lazy limbs of a five-legged donkey!"

Bou-Makari addressed this comment to a pair of scruffy young men leaning against the wall of a large *serai* and toying with harness leathers.

"Goods to show," he declared. "The best, you understand."

His assistants fell in after us as we entered a crowded eating room. Bou-Makari indicated that we should pass through it and make our way to the courtyard. We followed him down a covered walkway.

"Odd place for camels," Vesper muttered from the side of her mouth. "All of a sudden, I don't like this. What's he up to?"

"He would hardly attempt to rob us," I assured her. "Not in broad daylight."

"Forget the camels, Brinnie. Let's get out."

Vesper was about to turn around, but her instinct served us too late.

Her words hardly left her lips before Bou-Makari's colleagues sprang upon us from behind. At the same time, the camel trader wheeled and blocked us with his burly arms.

Vesper does not have the temperament to let herself be mauled without raising objections. She kicked furiously in all directions; one of the hirelings yelped in pain, but, despite her efforts, harness leathers were lashed around our wrists. We were hauled roughly along the passageway, down a flight of steps, and flung headlong into a lightless, vile-smelling chamber. The door was slammed and bolted behind us.

"Dear girl," I gasped, "we are not being robbed; we are being kidnapped!"

Vesper wasted no breath in reply, but immediately set about trying to untie my bonds. I attempted to do the same for her. Useless. The knots held fast.

Finally, exhausted, we gave up, and I sank down on the stone floor. The chamber was pitch dark, but Vesper located the door and, from there, inched her way along the walls. No doubt she hoped to find some other exit or even some discarded object that might serve us. Except for the odor, our cell held nothing.

"We have to think of how to get out of here," Vesper said. "The only trouble is, it's impossible."

"Then we have no hope!" I cried. If Vesper admitted defeat, we were surely lost.

"No," said Vesper. "Sooner or later, they'll have to do something with us. Give us food or water. They've kidnapped us, but they can't intend to starve us to death. But they're the ones who'll have to open that door. When they do— Well, I don't know yet. We'll wait and see.

"Don't forget, Brinnie, Bou-Makari thinks we're alone. He doesn't know about Maleesh and the twins. They must be looking for us this very moment."

I could not share her optimism. Though she urged me to rest and conserve my strength, I was unable to follow her advice. My wrists ached, and my heart even more. Vesper stretched out beside me, silent. How long we remained thus, I did not know, for I had lost all track of time.

Indeed, I had lost all hope as well. Vesper had been correct, but only to a limited extent. Eventually, our captors did come for us. If Vesper had contemplated escape at that instant, she had no chance to do so. We were quickly and efficiently dragged from our cellar chamber, hustled up the steps, and shoved into an open courtyard.

"At least we're outdoors again," Vesper whispered. "That's an improvement."

The sun blinded me for a moment. We had, I calculated, suffered a night of captivity, and it was now mid-morning. Vesper glanced around in surprise.

"What's all this?" she murmured. "Who are they?"

Some dozen or more men stood about in the courtyard, all of them very richly dressed. I would have guessed them to be merchants or travelers of substance, indeed, of large wealth, judging from the rings on their fingers and the gems in their turbans. My heart rose.

"Gentlemen!" I burst out. "Help us! We are Philadelphians, abducted, held against our will!"

"I don't think they care about that," muttered Vesper.

To my horror, they observed us impassively. Not one of them lifted a finger on our behalf. The disgusting Bou-Makari clapped his hands and urged them to draw closer.

"See for yourselves," he called out. "I spoke truth when I invited you here. Can there be finer merchandise? But only one of you will be rich enough to afford it. Who shall it be?"

Vesper turned to me. "Brinnie, we're not being kidnapped. We're being sold."

6

"I wonder," Vesper mused, "what's the going price for a *roumi* slave in Tizi Bekir?"

"Sell us?" I burst out. "Impossible! It is against the law!"

As indeed it was. The French had forbidden that abominable trade years before our late lamented President Lincoln had emancipated slaves from their bondage in our freedom-loving Union. To find the vilest of human transactions in a land governed by a republic whose proud motto was Liberty, Equality, Fraternity—no, this went beyond belief.

Nevertheless, Bou-Makari's assistants had hauled out a wooden bench and forced us to mount it. The disgusting camel trader continued to encourage the onlookers.

"Open wide your purses!" he cried. "Be generous in what you offer for this emerald-eyed gazelle, this fairest flower in the garden of beauty. The other one I give you free of charge."

"This is outrageous!" I flung at him. "Intolerable!"

"Brinnie, be quiet," Vesper suggested. "Make a fuss and they'll gag you. Just don't do anything. When we see what we have to deal with, we'll deal with it."

Vesper said no more, but held her head high, her glance unwavering. I tried to follow her example even when a couple of Bou-Makari's customers strolled over to inspect us.

"The maiden alone is worth a thousand gold pieces," remarked one of them, looking Vesper up and down and hardly giving me a moment's observation.

"A thousand?" retorted his bejeweled and ostentatiously dressed companion. "My first bid will be twice that!"

The nauseating Bou-Makari, smelling his fortune already made, broke in.

"Patience, my masters. You shall each have your chance. Let us now begin in proper fashion."

Bou-Makari signaled that the auction was ready to start.

"I offer the first bid."

The voice from the back of the crowd rose no louder than a tone of quiet conversation, but all in the courtyard—including Bou-Makari—fell instantly silent. Bowing deeply, the would-be bidders drew aside, leaving him a clear path.

The individual producing this effect stood a full head taller than any in the courtyard. He walked toward us—rather, he padded like a tiger, with noiseless, loose-limbed strides. Glancing neither left nor right, he paid no attention whatever to the respectful salaams. He seemed used to this kind of reception and took it for granted.

At his side hung a straight, two-edged sword, and slung over his shoulder, a long-barreled musket. A dagger in a leather sheath was bound to his left forearm. In brief, he was a walking arsenal. Yet, even without this array of weapons, he would have been a commanding figure.

"Brinnie," Vesper whispered, "he's blue!"

Blue indeed he was. Stained by the indigo pigments used to dye his belted tunic and trousers, his skin had absorbed their coloration, so that even his hands were blue. His face likewise, as much as could be seen of it; for he wore his blue turban with an end of it veiling most of his features. But it was this veil, more than his complexion, that set him so strikingly apart, as if it hid some unfathomable mystery. I confess that my blood ran a little cold—not only with fear but fascination.

Vesper must have sensed his magnetic force, too. Whoever or whatever he was, she could not take her eyes off him. Nor could anyone else in the courtyard.

For many long moments, he stood silent, his arms folded. He appeared accustomed to looking out across great distances; even when he fixed a searching gaze on Vesper, it was both intense and remote. And altogether inscrutable.

Bou-Makari, meantime, was smiling and salaaming and practically knocking his head in the dust.

The blue stranger gave an almost imperceptible nod. "May I be permitted to name the first price?"

Bou-Makari murmured that it would be an honor.

The man reached into the leather sack at his belt. And brought out one copper coin.

Bou-Makari choked a little.

Our would-be purchaser swung around to face the

crowd. He held up the coin for all to see. His hands were long and slender, surprisingly delicate. They also looked capable of doing highly disagreeable things to people, if necessary.

"This much I offer. Who offers more?"

Dead silence. The blue man waited patiently, eyes going from one face to another. No one moved a muscle, let alone raised the bid.

"Nothing higher? Speak now, once for all."

Bou-Makari's smile had frozen into a yellowish grin as the blue man continued, "What, among all you masters of riches, possessors of treasure, will none bid more than my humble copper coin?" He turned to Bou-Makari. "My price stands, then."

Bou-Makari began opening and closing his mouth in a fishlike manner. Beads of sweat covered his face.

"You seem ill at ease with our bargain." The blue man turned his glance from Bou-Makari to the silent onlookers. "Have I not observed the rule of the marketplace? Does one of you disagree? If so, come forward. Let us discuss the matter."

No one took up his invitation. I could hardly blame them.

"So be it. Judged and accepted by all," the blue man said quietly. "Bring them now to me."

Bou-Makari gave a few stifled wheezes. Whether choking from rage or fear, he was not a happy man. He managed to nod in feeble agreement and gestured to his henchmen, who fell all over themselves in their haste to help us down from the bench.

The blue man tossed his coin into the dust at Bou-Makari's feet and motioned for us to follow him. The crowd fell back to let us pass. Bou-Makari looked daggers, but made no attempt to stop us. Vesper cast him a pleasant smile.

Our owner—as, in the technical sense, he was—led us a little distance away. Satisfied that we were well out of Bou-Makari's reach, Vesper stopped in her tracks.

"You bought us," she said, "but we aren't for sale."

She went on to introduce us, explaining our purpose and the treachery that had put us in the camel dealer's clutches.

"I am An-Jalil," replied our purchaser, his blue veil hiding his expression. "An-Jalil es-Siba."

"I'm sure you'll understand," said Vesper. "In my country, we don't buy and sell people."

"But you are in *my* country," replied An-Jalil. "Yes, the French have outlawed slavery. Yet there are some who disobey our masters. In many ways."

"My good sir," I put in, "we shall gladly reimburse you for your expenses, plus any inconvenience—"

An-Jalil's eyes blazed. "You offer me payment?"

"Forgive Brinnie," Vesper said. "It's nothing against you personally, but—"

The blue man snatched out his dagger so quickly I never saw his hand move, and heard only the terrible hiss of the blade.

7

What a blessing that it was over quickly, before Vesper so much as blinked. Usually, the dear girl is remarkably nimble, but, in this case, her least movement might have spoiled An-Jalil's aim—with disastrous results. The keen blade merely whispered through the tough leather without even grazing her skin. I shut my eyes and held my breath while he sliced through my own bonds in a single—fortunately accurate—stroke.

"Take your freedom, *anisah.*" An-Jalil sheathed his dagger. He bowed slightly and swept a hand from his heart to his lips and brow.

"Thank you." Vesper gave him her most gracious smile.

"Do not thank me for returning what was already yours," An-Jalil replied. "I make no claim upon you or your companion. Did you believe I would have done so against your will?"

"We didn't mean to offend you," said Vesper, rubbing

her wrists. "It's just that we don't want to be owned. Not by anybody."

"You speak only truth, *anisah.* 'Even the slenderest chains weigh heavy.' So it is written."

" 'I thought myself free until I contemplated the eagle,' " returned Vesper, finishing the quotation. Naturally, she recognized those lines by ar-Ramadi, the illustrious twelfth-century Moorish poet.

An-Jalil's eyes glinted; with surprise or pleasure, I could not judge. Afraid he might launch more verses, I suggested it was unwise to linger in the vicinity.

"Sir," I said, "you have been our benefactor, no doubt at some risk to yourself. But we, too, are still at risk."

"That's right," said Vesper. "Bou-Makari wasn't overjoyed having his merchandise sold off at a bargain price. He'll try to get even."

"He will not trouble you," An-Jalil said.

Given that assurance, Vesper was in no hurry to return to our *serai.* I was. Our narrow escape had left me unnerved. Also, something teased the back of my mind, but I was too muddled to make sense of it.

"My dear sir, we must be on our way," I told him. "I do not know how to express our gratitude. With all respect, if there is any service we might render to you, we shall gladly do what we can."

"Be of service to yourselves," An-Jalil said. "You spoke of journeying to Bel-Saaba? Go not. I warn you against it."

"We won't turn back after we've come this far," said Vesper. "Why? What can you tell us?"

Before An-Jalil could reply, joyful shouts rose from the

top of the street. Maleesh, waving his arms, pelted toward us. Beside him ran Smiler and Slider. A little distance behind marched a detachment of French troops: Foreign Legionnaires in blue coats and white trousers. White cloth havelocks were fitted on their caps to shade their necks from the sun. They carried bayonetted rifles at the ready.

Vesper hurried to meet the twins and Maleesh.

"Safe and sound, are you?" Smiler beamed with delight and relief. "We've been hunting for you since yesterday. You might say we turned the place upside down, in all senses of the word."

"We did a good bit of turning," added Smiler, "and a fair amount of shaking where it seemed called for. But it's Mr. Maleesh who deserves the credit."

Maleesh grinned proudly. "While these twin gazelles of the mountains sought you by strength of their arms, I discovered what had befallen you. By this"—he tapped his ear—"which heard gossip in the bazaar. And this"—he touched his mouth—"to ask a question here and there. I learned of slaves offered only to the richest buyers. One was a chalice of burnished gold set with emeralds and pearls. The other—forgive me, Sidi Bahrini—an old crock. I knew it must be you."

"I was sure you'd find us sooner or later," Vesper said. "Twins, you must have done quite a job of shaking and turning. Maleesh, that was clever of you. Now, here's someone I'd like you to meet."

She turned to present An-Jalil.

He was gone. Our blue benefactor had vanished.

"But—where did he go?" Vesper's face fell. "We hardly thanked him properly."

By now, the French officer had approached us. Saluting, he introduced himself as Colonel Marelle. His men, he explained, had arrived in Tizi Bekir that morning. Maleesh had urged him to form a rescue party.

"It would seem, mademoiselle, that our services were not required."

Colonel Marelle, heavyset, with a sun-blackened face and a scrubby, pepper-and-salt mustache, had the hard-bitten air expected in one of his profession. But he gave Vesper a smile that was half humorous, half ironic. "Alas, the Legion is deprived of the honor of rescuing—how says one in English?—the damsel in distress."

Vesper thanked him nonetheless. I suggested that Colonel Marelle could at least have the honor of arresting the treacherous camel dealer and clapping him in irons immediately.

"I shall do so, of course," Marelle replied, "if you and Mademoiselle Holly insist."

We certainly did insist, I told him. Such an outrage could not go unpunished. Marelle raised a hand.

"Allow me to explain our situation. Come, let us take first a little refreshment. Mademoiselle Holly, you have denied me a rescue. Do not deny me the pleasure of your company."

Vesper gladly accepted. Marelle dismissed his men, and we walked back to the bazaar. Seeing us in safe hands, Maleesh and the twins headed for our quarters, while the colonel led us to a table in one of the open-fronted eating houses. Having nearly been auctioned off as a slave a short while before only put a finer edge on the dear girl's excellent appetite. While she absorbed melon slices and ripe figs, Marelle began:

"We do all possible to stamp out this abominable traffic." He had taken off his cap, revealing gray hair shaven almost to the bone, and leaned back in his chair. "Yet, it persists to some extent in these backlands. Sooner or later, we shall do away with it completely. For the moment, it is the better part of wisdom to look the other way.

"We are few in Jedera. The tribes outnumber us. If they ever cease to squabble among themselves and join together, they will drive us into the sea. Yet, La France desperately requires money. I am not proud to say this, but Jedera is our milk cow—who must be milked very delicately or she will kick the bucket."

"Kick over the bucket," Vesper gently corrected. "Kick the bucket means 'to die.'"

"It comes to the same. So it is my first duty to avoid trouble and not to stir it up or seek it out. It is a practical policy. For myself, I would prefer it if the French were not here at all. But I am an officer. Above all, an officer of the Legion. I command. Also, I obey."

This attitude struck me as unusual. Most of the colonials I had met during my travels set the natives an example of European civilization by brutalizing them. Marelle, as Vesper drew him out a little more, was not usual.

She soon learned that he had been born in Mokarra of a Jederan mother and French father, that he was fluent in all the tribal dialects, and that his devotion to Jedera was as fierce as his devotion to his beloved Legion. He was the sort of fellow who should be a governor-general and seldom is.

When Colonel Marelle finished his account of himself, Vesper told him all that had happened to us. After she described our benefactor, the colonel appeared greatly impressed.

"You have had the rare privilege of meeting a Tawarik, the most ancient and unyielding of all the tribes. Depending on the season, they tent in the Haggar, but prefer to roam the desert. From what you say of him, he was an *eggali,* the noblest caste of knightly warriors."

"His name," said Vesper, "was An-Jalil es-Siba."

Marelle's eyebrows went halfway up his forehead. "An *eggali?* The *amenokal* himself! The veritable chieftain of the Tawarik! Do you understand the word *es-Siba?* It means 'the unsubmitting.' He is well named."

"You know him?" asked Vesper.

"By reputation. I have never seen him. Until now, we have chosen to avoid each other. How do you say it? An agreement between gentlemen. But, recently, I have reports that he hopes to rally the tribes against us. Not only in the mountains but the towns. It is rumored that he was, not long ago, in Mokarra."

"So he was!" I exclaimed. Suddenly it came clear to me. Though without the burnoose, An-Jalil had the same stride, the same bearing. When I told this to Vesper, she gave a perplexed frown.

"Do you think he was following us? Why should he? Was it only a coincidence?"

"I cannot guess his purpose regarding you, mademoiselle," put in the colonel. "As far as it concerns us, he could pose the greatest threat to our authority. Thus, it is my sworn duty to arrest him if possible, shoot him if necessary.

"And yet"—Marelle smiled regretfully—"for myself, I

41

wish I might meet him face-to-face, man-to-man. He is a worthy opponent, a most gallant enemy."

"For us, he was a gallant friend," said Vesper. "Do you know why he warned us against Bel-Saaba?"

Marelle shook his head. "I have no information. But I have advice. When es-Siba gives a warning, heed it."

Vesper, I could tell from a certain look in her eyes, had no intention of doing so. She let Marelle's comment pass and took up another subject. During his conversation, the colonel had spoken of leading his men to Fort Iboush. Vesper, offhandedly, questioned him about it.

"It is a small fortress," Marelle replied. "We keep a garrison there only as a matter of principle. A question of showing the flag. It is at the edge of the Sahkra. We do not patrol beyond it."

"It's on the way to Bel-Saaba, isn't it?" Vesper asked innocently.

"More or less. Fort Iboush is a little to the east of the pass. As one reaches the desert—" Marelle broke off and gave Vesper a sidelong glance. "Ah, mademoiselle, you try clever tactics on an old soldier. Logic tells me you wish to accompany us. Your charm tells me you intend to persuade me. *Non,* I cannot allow it."

"I should have known I couldn't outmaneuver a Legionnaire." Vesper shrugged. "Too bad. If you can't, you can't. Just for the sake of argument, though, you'll admit we'd be safer traveling with you."

"Unquestionably. Two things, however, make it impossible." Marelle held up one finger. "First, we must be en route within the hour. You are not prepared. You have not sufficient animals or equipment." He raised another

42

finger. "Second, you could not keep up with my troops. You have never seen the Legion on the march? If forced, we go as fast as cavalry; in bad terrain, faster. It is a matter of pride with us."

Vesper, in her turn, raised a finger.

"Point one, suppose Brinnie could get all our equipment together before you leave." She added another finger. "Point two, suppose we could keep up the pace."

"You suppose a great deal," said Marelle.

"Point three," Vesper went on, "suppose we didn't insist on arresting Bou-Makari and just called the matter closed. It seems to me I showed more fingers than you did."

Colonel Marelle laughed in spite of himself. "Mademoiselle Holly, I expected you to assault me with charm. Instead, you wish to conquer by arithmetic. *Très bien,* I challenge you. Meet my conditions and you shall accompany us."

Vesper was correct to the extent that Marelle's troops would be a safe escort. For myself, I would have settled for the arrest of Bou-Makari. With the best will in the world, I could not assemble all we needed in so short a time.

But before any further discussion could take place, we were interrupted by Maleesh dashing up to our table.

"Anisah!" he shouted. "Come and see! Six camels are standing at our gate. With harness, saddles, everything! Chests of clothing, boxes of food, skins of water!"

"Whose are they?" Vesper jumped to her feet. "Can we buy them right now?"

"They are yours!" cried Maleesh. "A gift from the

heavens! No, not the heavens. The boys who brought them said they came from Bou-Makari."

"Take it all back," I ordered, in spite of Vesper's jubilant cry. "We accept nothing from that scoundrel. How does he have the gall to send us a gift? Return everything to him immediately."

"But that cannot be done," replied Maleesh. "I am told that Bou-Makari is gone. Where, it is not known. He is not expected in Tizi Bekir again."

Vesper grinned at Colonel Marelle and held up two fingers.

"Voilà," she said. "Point one. And point three."

Regarding Vesper's point two, Colonel Marelle could have flatly refused to let us go with him. He was, perhaps, too much the gallant Frenchman to break his agreement, though surely he was as astonished as I by the miraculous arrival of supplies and transport. More likely, the hard-bitten Legionnaire had simply found himself outflanked and hopelessly bamboozled by the dear girl—as had others before him.

The camels, in any case, were excellent, probably Bou-Makari's private stock. I suspected that An-Jalil had something to do with their sudden appearance, but I wondered what sort of persuasion he had exercised.

"Don't look a gift camel in the mouth," said Vesper.

While Smiler and Slider packed our belongings, Maleesh took charge of the animals. Our horses and mules, he assured us, would be well suited to the mountain trails. He advised us to ride the horses, keeping the mules and camels for pack beasts.

Maleesh again proved remarkably competent and efficient. From Bou-Makari's bales of clothing, he picked out sturdy garb for Vesper and me: tunics and trousers, tough-soled but comfortable boots. Under his leadership, harnesses were buckled, boxes and chests roped, and loads balanced with amazing speed.

Thanks to him, we stood ready to depart a good fifteen minutes before Marelle's troops put themselves in marching order. The colonel, astride a stocky, deep-chested horse, gave Vesper an admiring salute.

"Mademoiselle Holly, you have my felicitations and compliments. For the moment."

We left the town and almost immediately found ourselves engaged in the first ascents of Tizi Bekir and an abrupt change of landscape. The caravan route itself was fairly smooth, after a thousand or so years of traffic, but the slopes rising on either side of us were bleakly depressing, bare except for scattered clumps of stunted vegetation. Towering above us, the black crags of the Haggar, grim and looking hard as iron, were streaked with dazzling white snow.

As we wended our way, Vesper's thoughts turned to An-Jalil. "I'm sorry I didn't see more of him. I understand why he disappeared when Colonel Marelle showed up. For the rest, it puzzles me."

It puzzled me, as well. A blue-tinted individual who goes around armed to the teeth and quoting twelfth-century poetry is not easy to comprehend. Yet, I admit I shared Vesper's fascination with him.

Caught up in the intriguing subject of An-Jalil, Vesper only now realized that Marelle's Legionnaires had outdistanced us. Maleesh hurried back to instill some enthusiasm in our camels. We put our mounts into a brisk trot in order to catch up.

Colonel Marelle, riding back and forth along the column, flashed a hard grin.

"Recall to yourself point two," he called. "Keep pace."

He wheeled his horse about. I assured Vesper that the colonel, having taken us this far, would not leave us in the lurch.

Next thing we knew, in spite of their heavy packs, the detachment broke into double-quick time, with Marelle still grinning and waving at us to follow.

We urged our horses to a faster pace, but it was all we could do to keep the gap between our caravan and the Legion column from widening. Maleesh, Smiler, and Slider rode up to us to learn the cause of the sudden speed.

"Marelle's sticking to his bargain," said Vesper. "I'll do the same."

There was a gleam in her eyes, but I did not grasp the full significance of her remark until she sprang down from the saddle.

"They're going on foot," said Vesper. "So will I."

She strode quickly to join the rear of the column.

"The *anisah* marches?" exclaimed Maleesh. "Then must I stay by her side."

Dismounting, he ran to overtake Vesper. The twins looked at each other.

"I don't see as how we can let those Frenchies outdo us," declared Smiler.

"I don't see as how we can let Miss Vesper take them on without, you might say, our moral support," replied Slider.

The pair nodded identically, jumped from their mounts and, keeping exact step with each other, trotted after the Legionnaires.

Though tempted to follow, I suppressed that impulse. True, a point of honor and possibly the reputation of Philadelphia were at stake. On the other hand, our untended pack animals had begun wandering off the trail. Someone had to herd the unruly beasts into line.

By the time I came in sight of Marelle and his troops, the Legionnaires had mercifully halted. In the midst of them stood Vesper, slightly flushed but scarcely winded, laughing and joking, a Legionnaire's cap and havelock perched on her head.

Marelle, mopping his brow, came up to greet me.

"I have not played fair with Mademoiselle Holly," he confessed. "What you saw was our famous forced-march pace. We do it only in dire emergency, but here I could not resist a little test of her resolution. Which she passed with full marks."

"Too bad you weren't along, Brinnie," Vesper said. "Wonderful exercise."

From then on, we proceeded at a comfortably normal speed. At many points, though, we seemed to be heading back toward Tizi Bekir. This was because the increasing steepness of the mountains made straight progress impossible, so we followed long switchbacks and looping trails.

Vesper chose to continue on foot with the Legionnaires, who had adopted her as something of a mascot. The twins, feeling that they had sufficiently upheld American honor, stayed on horseback. Maleesh, however, marched at Vesper's side and showed an endurance equal to hers.

Thus we continued for several days, tenting wherever we found level ground, often sleeping under the enormous stars, our burnooses wrapped around us.

As for provisions, Colonel Marelle insisted that we share the Legion's rations and save our own against future need.

A thoughtful gesture, but eventually disastrous. For me, in any case.

One evening my helping of tinned beef was of dubious taste and color. By the next morning, chills convulsed me and I could barely speak.

"Brinnie, you've gone all green." Vesper put a hand on my forehead. Her face turned grave.

Colonel Marelle arrived with his medical orderly, who glumly shook his head. I dimly gathered that my condition required more treatment than the Legion could provide.

By then, I was past caring.

After conferring briefly with Colonel Marelle, Vesper came to kneel beside me. "We're taking you to a doctor."

In my fevered condition, I murmured that we had no appointment.

"Maleesh says we should turn off the trail and find a village," Vesper said. "We're going to do that."

"There will surely be a *tabib*," put in Maleesh, "wise in all ways of medicine."

"Here's a place just above us, in this upland valley." Vesper studied the colonel's map and traced a route with her finger. "It's very close. We can carry you easily and have you there in no time."

For all their desolation, these reaches of the Haggar held populations larger than one might expect. The key, of course, was water. A stream of any size always had a village nearby, with sheep and goats grazing in the little stretches of meadowland.

"That's it, then," declared Vesper. "We'll go to—what's it called? 'Ait-Ouzrim'?"

"No, no!" cried Maleesh. "Choose another, not Ait-Ouzrim. Anywhere, *anisah,* anywhere but there!"

"What's wrong?" asked Vesper. "It's the closest. Aren't the villagers friendly?"

"Very friendly," Maleesh replied. "They welcome all travelers. It is the tribal law of hospitality. Yes, they will feed and house you as honored guests."

"Well, if there's no danger—"

"No danger to you," said Maleesh. "To me. Woe unto your servant! Ait-Ouzrim is the village of the Beni-Brahim."

"Beni whatever," said Vesper, "as long as they have a doctor."

"You do not understand, *anisah.* I am a Beni-Hareet. The Beni-Brahim have fought my tribe for centuries, in hatred passed down from generation to generation. You they will honor, feast, give cushions to sit upon, anoint you with fragrant oils. Me—they will chop into small pieces. Sheik Addi, their leader, will kill me on sight."

"I see what you mean," said Vesper. "All right, you can go with Colonel Marelle and meet us later. Or stay in the hills for a while."

Maleesh brightened at this. Then he hesitated and finally shook his head. "Our fortunes are linked. So it is written. So it must be. I have sworn to stay by your side. Whatever befalls me, my spirit will look down upon you from the stars and guide you on your path."

"Hold on a minute before you start looking down from the stars," Vesper said. "This Sheik Addi—he knows you're a Beni-Hareet?"

"No, he has never laid eyes on me," said Maleesh. "The Beni-Hareet and the Beni-Brahim have hardly seen each other—only at shooting distance, over their rifle sights."

"Well, then, you don't have to let on. If anyone asks who you are, you're just my servant, you came with us from Mokarra. That's the truth—in a way."

Maleesh rubbed his jaw for a while, then nodded. "So be it. If you say I am your servant from Mokarra, none should question further."

Colonel Marelle agreed with Vesper's plan, and promised to wait on the trail until he had word we were safe in Ait-Ouzrim. The twins fabricated a stretcher from some of our tent canvas and hoisted me onto it while Maleesh put our caravan in order. Vesper said a grateful farewell to the colonel, and we set out for the village.

Sighting us well before our arrival, a number of villagers swarmed out to welcome us and lead us to a little square in the midst of flat-roofed, white-plaster houses.

Vesper, wasting no time on formalities, immediately asked for a *tabib* to help us. Fortunately, that professional gentleman happened to be in the crowd. He stepped forward and listened carefully as Vesper explained my misfortune.

Except for the turban and striped caftan, the *tabib* had the same air of stern yet noble dedication as our illustrious clinician, Dr. Samuel Gross. He poked and prodded, squinted down my throat and up my nose, all the while muttering to himself as incomprehensibly as our finest Philadelphia specialists. Finally, he pronounced a solemn prognosis.

"I cannot cure him."

Vesper cried out in dismay, but the *tabib* continued.

"No, I cannot cure him. Nor do I need to. He must cure himself, as he will surely do."

He went on to explain that my illness was rarely fatal. I required rest, sparse diet, and herbal infusions he would provide. Time, he assured us, was my best medicine.

By now, Sheik Addi himself had arrived. That is, he rolled up, for he was almost as wide as he was tall, plump-cheeked, with a turban twice the size of his head. His eyes lit up at sight of Vesper, while he greeted us in a voice like a bull calf.

As soon as Vesper told him our situation, he herded us all into his residence, a large house bursting with children of assorted sizes. While his three wives hurried to welcome us, Sheik Addi bawled for his eldest daughter, Jenna, to tend me. Smiler and Slider hauled me to a chamber, which Jenna set about arranging as a sick room.

Vesper took my hand. "Dear old Brinnie, you'll be good as new. The *tabib* says so. And I say so."

Vesper watched over and cared for me night and day. As did Jenna. A bright-eyed, handsome young woman with crimson cords tied in her shining black hair, she had natural skill as a nurse and healer. Thanks to her ministrations, and Vesper's, I gradually improved. Though unable to travel, by week's end I was up to taking short walks around the village. No longer confined to my sick room, I was welcomed into Sheik Addi's family life: as loud and boisterous as the sheik himself, with his offspring clamoring and Addi hugging or swatting them, depending on his mood.

Vesper quickly became their favorite, telling them stories to which they listened wide-eyed. Sheik Addi was equally fascinated. One tale he liked especially dealt with the hero Paw el-Revere galloping on his camel to warn the sleeping Bou-Stoni tribe of enemy attack.

As for Smiler and Slider, they were viewed as objects of wonder. Twins being rare among the Beni-Brahim, they could not set foot outdoors without a crowd gathering.

Maleesh, however, outshone them. He had become as popular as Vesper among the villagers. Now confident he would not be chopped into bits, he basked in his reputation as a worldly-wise visitor from the capital. He strolled around Ait-Ouzrim, striking up conversations, drawing worshipful glances, holding forth in a respectful circle of his sworn, but unwitting, enemies. I give him credit: The fellow did have a way about him.

"He could get himself elected sheik," Vesper observed, "if they didn't have one already."

His popularity, however, did not extend to Jenna. With us, she was smiling, quick-witted, with a charming, silvery laugh. Yet I saw clearly that she and Maleesh had taken an instant dislike to each other. Jenna, indeed, went out of her way to demonstrate her low opinion of him; once, she even smacked him on the ear. Maleesh, in turn, behaved with utmost impudence. Instead of avoiding her, he sought her out with the express purpose of squabbling.

Most irritating for him, she refused to be impressed by his tricks—unlike Sheik Addi, who, along with the rest of his children, enjoyed them so much that he demanded Maleesh perform each evening.

Maleesh, I must admit, was at the top of his form. He danced on his hands more spectacularly than in Mokarra and turned incredible cartwheels and somersaults. His conjuring had never been so brilliantly mystifying. One evening, he presented his disappearing coin trick—with added improvements—finally tossing the copper piece high into the air, where it vanished.

The children cheered and clapped their hands, Sheik Addi's wives gasped in amazement, and Sheik Addi himself outdid all of them, stamping his feet, roaring approval, demanding more. Jenna remained unimpressed.

"The coin did not vanish," she said archly. "You did not throw it in the air, but only made it seem so."

"Are you also a magician, little *anisah*?" Maleesh bristled. "Tell me, then, where it is."

"In your sleeve," retorted Jenna. "One does not need to be a magician to know that."

Maleesh snorted a denial. Jenna, nevertheless, kept at him, daring him to prove his claim. Maleesh, growing more and more vexed, finally gave a cry of exasperation and pushed both sleeves up to his shoulders.

Jenna gasped. Sheik Addi's eyes bulged and his plump cheeks went purple. Maleesh himself stared around, horrified at what he had thoughtlessly revealed.

On his forearm was a brightly colored, intricately designed tattoo.

"Beni-Hareet!" Sheik Addi jumped to his feet, no longer roaring with delight but rage. "The tribal mark of the Beni-Hareet!"

Maleesh clapped his hands to his head, cursing himself for being goaded into such carelessness. Jenna covered her face and rocked back and forth. The children stared, puzzled by the whole affair.

"Guards! Here!" Sheik Addi spat and shook a fist at

Maleesh. As his men raced in answer to his call, Addi pulled a dagger from the sash around his waist.

"Vile swine of a Beni-Hareet!" he bellowed. "Kill him! Strike him down! No! Let me at him first!"

10

"No! You can't!" Vesper had jumped to her feet as quickly as Sheik Addi to set herself squarely in front of him. Smiler and Slider planted themselves on either side of her, and I, despite my weakened condition, stumbled to join them.

Sheik Addi only responded with a growl of rage. Brandishing his dagger, he prepared to carve his way through Vesper and all the rest of us to get at the terrified Maleesh. Addi's guards hesitated, uncertain what to do.

"We're all guests in your village, in your home, under your roof," cried Vesper. "Break the law of hospitality? Harm one of us and you'll be disgraced forever."

It was a delicate moment. Vesper, hands on hips, boldly facing the infuriated sheik, had no intention of giving ground, and Addi, eyes blazing, hulked forward until he was practically nose to nose with her. His wives tipped the balance in our favor. They flung themselves on him and pulled him back.

"The *anisah* speaks truth!" one of them shouted.

"Hospitality is sacred. Shame yourself, you shame us with you."

Jenna added her voice to the protest while the children, alarmed by such behavior from their elders, cried and screamed. All this kept Addi from carrying out his purpose then and there but did nothing to soothe him.

"The law does not shield this maggot!" he bellowed. "Hospitality? No! Not for one of the Beni-Hareet!"

"Not a member in good standing," Maleesh piped up from behind his screen of legs.

"Worm!" Addi waved his dagger. "You were born a Beni-Hareet; you die as one."

"Wait a minute, Addi," put in Vesper. "You admit the law applies to us?"

"I have no quarrel with you," Sheik Addi flung back. "Only with this mange-ridden goat, this polluter of the oasis of my life, this blight on the fig tree of my generosity."

"We're under your protection, then," said Vesper.

"So I have spoken. So it is."

"All right, if we're under your protection, Maleesh is under ours. That means he's under yours, too," Vesper went on. "Things equal to the same thing are equal to each other. It's one of Euclid's unbreakable laws."

"Who is this Euclid?" retorted Addi. "He means nothing to me."

"I'll put it another way," said Vesper. "You wouldn't destroy our property, would you? Of course not. I don't mean that we own Maleesh. But we hired him. So, you could say we own his time. You can't separate his time from him, can you? If his time is our property, Maleesh is our property, too."

Addi's wives and Jenna murmured approval of Vesper's lucid exposition. Addi scowled, chewed his lips, pulled off his turban, flung it to the ground, and stamped on it. Of more immediate interest to us, he put his dagger—reluctantly—back into his sash.

"Your property? So be it. He is no more than a saddle blanket, a camel's nose bag. Let him stay with the rest of your animals." Addi spun around to his wives. "Out! Out! All of you!"

Maleesh hastily obeyed. The women bundled up the smallest children and shooed the others from the room. His face turning a variety of colors, Addi stamped after them, kicking at the cushions on the floor as he stormed out. Jenna stayed behind.

"What have I done?" She threw herself into Vesper's arms. "I did not mean to put him in danger."

"For heaven's sake, then, why did you prod him like that? Why did you want to spoil his trick?"

"Not to spoil it. To make it better. I knew the coin would not be in his sleeve. He is too clever for that. I only wished to make him show it was not there, as some might have thought, so his trick would be all the more astonishing."

"He'll be fine," Vesper assured her. "Don't feel bad. You meant well. Besides, he's only a Beni-Hareet."

"We women have no quarrel with the Beni-Hareet. Our men keep it alive, not us."

"Oh?" said Vesper. "Well, they've been keeping it alive a good long time."

"Beyond memory," said Jenna. "No one is even sure who began it. There was, long ago, an upland pasture. The Beni-Hareet claimed it as their own. The Beni-Brahim claimed their grandsires owned it centuries before. The Beni-Hareet then claimed their great-grandsires held it first, and the Beni-Brahim swore their great-great-grandsires were first to graze their flocks there."

"And no one knows who it belonged to?"

"It belonged to both," said Jenna. "The Beni-Brahim and the Beni-Hareet descend from two brothers of the same father. The tribes were cousins to one another. Now they are mortal enemies.

"Do you believe we women worry about great-great-grandsires?" Jenna went on. "Year upon year, the village mothers see their sons' blood shed without reason. The pasture is long since fallow and useless. The men fight over what is dead and gone. Our concern is for the living."

"At least you don't have to grieve over Maleesh," Vesper said. "He's safe now. We'll leave as soon as we can."

The sooner the better, was my opinion. Smiler and Slider immediately offered to build an improved stretcher, or a horse litter. Vesper shook her head.

"Brinnie, you're in no condition to be moved on a stretcher or any other way. We'll go when you quit looking so green around the gills. The Beni-Brahim will get used to having a Beni-Hareet in their village."

Vesper was a little too optimistic. While she and the twins lost none of their popularity during the following days, it was not so with Maleesh. Word had spread. At this point, the wretched fellow could not have been elected dogcatcher.

Worse yet, Sheik Addi took Vesper at her exact words.

If Maleesh was property, he had no reason to eat. "Does a saddle need food?" Addi demanded. "Does a piece of baggage need water?"

"You can't treat him worse than a mule or a camel," Vesper countered.

"So be it," Addi retorted. "He shall feed like a pack beast. Let him eat hay."

As things turned out, Addi's wives and Jenna saved their leftovers and sneaked them into the stable, which was now the residence of Maleesh. Our guide and protector did not venture to put his nose out of doors.

Sheik Addi treated us as usual. That is to say, some days he would sulk, pout, glare silently at Vesper; others, he would shower her with praise. The only consistent thing about him was his delight in Vesper's stories.

His eyes popped at her account of the great Ben-Jamin who summoned lightning from the heavens. He bellowed and slapped his knees over Samu el-Adams and the Bou-Stonis who painted their faces, put feathers in their hair, and cast boxes of mint tea into the harbor. Vesper told him of Ibn-Jeffer and Sheik el-Washington, of the mighty bell of Philad el-Phia, of Betsi ar-Ross stitching a banner from her caftan.

"I don't know if all those stories are good for him," Vesper remarked to me. "Addi only likes the parts with fighting. He doesn't pay much attention to the rest."

Our host, nevertheless, called for more and more, refusing to let an evening pass without a tale. To avoid sending Addi into a tantrum, Vesper indulged him, with some reluctance. By now, I felt well enough to travel, and Vesper was impatient for us to be on our way. Each time she mentioned that we were ready to leave, Addi waved away the idea, his eyes glinted dangerously, and he demanded still another story.

"I'll have to think of something he won't like at all," Vesper told me. "Something boring. The banking system? Fertilizer production?"

Finally, she simply announced our firm decision. We would leave the next day.

"Is that how you repay my hospitality?" Addi shouted. "You scorn my generosity! You fling my kindness in my face!"

"Addi, we're not scorning or flinging anything," Vesper patiently replied. "We're grateful to you. We just can't stay any longer."

"The others may depart," cried Addi. "Not you. No, I do not allow it. You remain until I give permission."

"That won't do," Vesper said. "We're going, all of us. If you force your hospitality on us, we might as well be prisoners."

Sheik Addi chewed on that for a while. Then a sly look crept over his face. "So be it. Go, if you wish."

"We'll start packing now," said Vesper.

"The Beni-Hareet stays here. Once you set foot beyond Ait-Ouzrim, that worm will no longer be under your protection. I shall deal with him as he deserves."

"Hold on, Addi," Vesper returned. "We've already settled that. Maleesh goes with us. He's ours; you agreed he was."

"No," retorted Addi. "You tricked me. I am not bound by deceit."

"Tricked you?" said Vesper. "How?"

"I do not know. That is proof of your trickery."

Sheik Addi grinned triumphantly over his masterpiece of logic and hunkered down solidly on his cushion. "You go. The worm stays. And dies."

Vesper thought for a while, then shrugged. "If you say so, I won't argue with you. All right, we'll leave Maleesh behind."

Smiler and Slider gasped identically, glancing at Vesper in disbelief, as, indeed, I myself did.

"That is wisdom." Addi bobbed his head, smiling and licking his lips at what he had in store for the wretched Maleesh.

"We'd better get a good night's sleep." Vesper yawned. "Oh—I do have one more story for you."

"The Bou-Stoni massacre?" Added leaned forward eagerly. "I would hear that told again."

"A different story." Vesper crossed her legs, settled on her cushion, and began in the tones of a bazaar storyteller:

"Hear, O Sheik! A man had a friend who set out on a journey, leaving in the man's care a chest of belongings.

"But, once his friend had mounted his camel and departed, the man laid hands on the chest and broke it to pieces. He tore the goods it held and trampled them underfoot. He burned the splintered chest and cast the ashes to the wind.

"When his friend returned and asked for the chest, the man said, 'Lo, I have destroyed it and all it contained.' His friend asked, 'Why have you done this to what was mine?' To which the man replied, 'Because the chest was offensive in my sight. Therefore, I did with it as I chose.' "

Addi waited for Vesper to continue. She folded her hands. "That's all there is to it."

"What?" shouted Addi. "The traveler took no revenge on his false friend? The destroyer of the chest—What man of honor would do such a vile deed? Monstrous! Unspeakable! That man is a wart on the nose of the universe! He should be cast out, his bones broken as he broke the chest! Can such a one truly exist?"

Vesper looked him squarely between the eyes. In the noble cadences of Second Samuel, Chapter Twelve, Verse Seven—the Authorized Version, of course—she declared:

" 'Thou art the man.' "

Addi jumped to his feet. "I? How dare you speak thus?"

"We're leaving our property behind," Vesper said. "Maleesh. You'll destroy him. Isn't a life, even a Beni-Hareet's, worth more than a chest? How are you different from the man in the tale? Hear your judgment from your own lips, O Sheik!"

Addi's plump cheeks went violet; he tore at his hair, pulled out his dagger, put it back again, clenched his fists and shook them in all directions. Vesper kept silent, while I feared he might come down with a fit.

"Go," he finally muttered in a choked voice. "Take the Beni-Hareet with you, to the depths of perdition. I will hear no more of that camel's nose bag, that flea, that descendant of cockroaches."

Vesper smiled at him. "I knew you'd be reasonable about it."

We left before the crack of dawn. The twins passed word to Maleesh, who had our gear already loaded. Ait-Ouzrim lay silent and deserted as we rode out. Maleesh, overjoyed at escaping with a whole skin, urged our camels to a faster pace.

With Ait-Ouzrim well behind us, Vesper ordered a

halt so that I could rest. Maleesh immediately set about hauling the roll of tenting down from the camel's back.

"We aren't going to camp yet," Vesper called. Maleesh paid no attention. She went over to him while he continued untying the ropes. "Maleesh, we don't need to pitch a tent now."

"*Anisah,* forgive me, but—" He unrolled the rest of the canvas.

Jenna scrambled out.

11

"I wish you'd talked to me first." Vesper held out her arms to Jenna. "You must have been half smothered in that canvas. And you, Maleesh, you should have told me ahead of time. I could have figured out something better."

So could I. Namely, seizing the idiot by the scruff of the neck and shaking him. If he had meant to take revenge by kidnapping a Beni-Brahim—an insane thing to do in the first place—he had compounded his rashness by abducting one who so despised him.

"My dear, dear Brinnie," Vesper said. "Jenna doesn't despise him. Don't you understand? I knew it from the start. They fell in love at first sight and had to do everything they could to make everyone think the opposite."

"That is truth, Sidi Bahrini." Maleesh looked half proud, half sheepish. "Forgive us, but no sooner did we set eyes on each other than I knew it was written: She is the flowering oasis of my heart, a fountain in the desert of my soul."

"And the pickle barrel of Addi's wrath," Vesper said. "When he realizes Jenna's missing, he has brains enough to put two and two together; easier, one and one."

Sheik Addi, I pointed out, would set after us with half Ait-Ouzrim. Had Maleesh given a passing thought to that? He and Jenna were gazing into each other's eyes. I doubted that they heard a word of what I said.

"We can be sure of what Addi's going to do," said Vesper. "The only question is: What are *we* going to do?"

"Have no fear." Maleesh disentangled himself from Jenna. "I have contemplated it carefully. We can keep on with all haste and hope to be safe in Bel-Saaba."

"And if Addi catches up with us before that?" returned Vesper. "He'll be on horseback, without baggage. He'll go faster than we can."

"I have thought of that, too," said Maleesh. "My second plan is this: We shall turn off the trail, hide, and wait for Sheik Addi and his followers to pass us by."

"Won't do," said Vesper. "If they don't see us ahead of them, they'll soon guess we're behind them. They'll comb the hills for us. Addi isn't the sort to give up easily."

"I have considered that, as well," replied Maleesh. "If it is our destiny, if it is written, they will find us."

Rather tartly I asked if he had considered what would happen after that? Romantic attachments, I have always observed, fog the mind and obscure sensible judgment.

"It is very simple, Sidi Bahrini," he said. "If Sheik Addi catches me, he will kill me for stealing his daughter. As for Jenna, he will only give her a beating and take her home."

"No," declared Jenna. "If he harms Maleesh, he must slay me first."

"Which is exactly what I won't let happen to either of you," said Vesper.

"We've had one or two brushes with unfriendly mobs," said Slider, as the twins had been listening to our conversation without appearing unduly upset by our plight. "I guess we can hold our own."

"We've had our little disagreements with highly aggravated Texans," added Smiler. "These Beni fellows can't be worse. We promise you, Miss Vesper, Slider and I will give a pretty fair account of ourselves."

"I know you will," said Vesper, "but that's what I want to avoid."

"I have one last plan," put in Maleesh. "Jenna and I have talked of it, but it is the least acceptable to me. Even so, I must speak it now. Our presence is your danger. We are the ones whom Sheik Addi seeks, not you."

"As long as you do not try to shield us," Jenna said, "my father will not harm you. He will bluster and rant, surely, but his vengeance is for us."

"In Jedera, I told you, *anisah,* that our destinies were bound together with a golden chain," added Maleesh. "So it was written, so it was. But now Jenna and I are bound with a stronger chain: the love in our hearts."

Maleesh dropped to his knees at Vesper's feet. "*Anisah,* I must ask you to break the link between you and me. I swore to be your servant and so I shall continue, if that is your will. Or, set me free of my word for the sake of my beloved.

"Jenna and I shall take leave of you here. We can hide more easily in the hills, only we two, and travel more quickly. We shall make our way to Mokarra. If we fail, if we should be captured, it will be our lives alone lost, not Sidi Bahrini's, not the twin moons'."

"Of course you're free." Vesper raised Maleesh to his feet. "I don't think your plan's all that good, but I haven't got a better one."

Jenna gratefully flung her arms around Vesper. Maleesh, looking resolute, embraced us and showered us with blessings. It was all very heartwarming, but, I pointed out to Vesper, the result was that we would now be in the middle of the Haggar without a guide.

Vesper did not find this distressing. "Do you still have Colonel Marelle's map?" she asked the twins.

"We do, miss," replied Slider.

"That's all we need," Vesper declared. "We can manage on our own."

Vesper insisted that Maleesh and Jenna take two horses and an ample share of provisions. We wasted no more time in extended farewells. The loving couple mounted and turned off the trail. Vesper watched as they disappeared into the uplands.

"Ait-Ouzrim isn't Verona," she said, "but Maleesh and Jenna make a good Romeo and Juliet."

I reminded her what happened to the star-crossed pair.

"That's only in the play," said Vesper.

As we set out again, Vesper turned unusually silent. She glanced back uneasily. I asked what was troubling her.

"I shouldn't have let Maleesh and Jenna go off by themselves," she finally answered. "They'd have been safer staying with us. Or would they? I just don't know if I did right or not."

I had never known her to be so uncertain. Her doubts made my own apprehensions worse, and I grew doubly nervous about our situation.

Indeed, the longer we continued on the trail the more I, too, wished Maleesh had remained. Without his organizing skill and his ability to hold our caravan together, our progress became slow and straggly. Dangerously so. Sheik Addi, I feared, would have no difficulty catching up with us. I found myself constantly listening for approaching hoofbeats.

Above all, I missed Maleesh because of the camels. In his absence, it became my duty to keep them in line and moving as rapidly as possible. He was more expert than I in dealing with the reluctant beasts. He had a way with them, much as he had with the villagers before his downfall. The creatures sensed an unfamiliar hand and turned rambunctious, trying to shake off their loads, so that I had to trot along on foot, giving each my personal attention.

The animal kingdom is untainted by the deliberate malice found so often in our human species. The camel is an exception. I soon grew convinced that our camels had conspired among themselves to make my life miserable. One spat on me while another tried to kick me. As the trail grew steeper and narrower, they reared and tossed their heads and constantly attempted to crowd me against the rocky wall rising to one side.

We had begun passing through the highest reaches of Tizi Bekir, where the trail fell sharply away as it followed the edge of a deep ravine. I had to goad the camel ahead of me to move forward while I pulled at the harness of the one behind.

As I did so, the beast lowered its long neck and gave me such a nip that, avoiding another attack, I sprang aside, stumbled, and lost my footing.

With the creature's gleeful snort ringing in my ears, I pitched headlong toward the ravine.

12

My exasperation at being so maliciously treated by the camel quickly gave way to concern for my life as I tumbled toward the bottom of the ravine, slipping and sliding, buffeted by outcroppings of sharp rocks. Clawing desperately at the side of the cliff, I finally halted my descent midway between the trail above and the dry riverbed below. I did not dare to move. Each time I sought a firmer handhold, the stones gave way, obliging me to cling there, frozen to the spot.

My persistent shouting had alerted Vesper to my difficulties. I glimpsed her, with Slider and Smiler, peering at me and distantly heard them encouraging me to hold on. I did so, having no better choice.

After a few moments, a rope fell dangling before me. Vesper called down, telling me to harness it under my arms. She soon realized I could not loosen my grip to follow her instructions, and, after several extremely long moments, she came scrambling to my side, well attached to the end of another cord.

"Brinnie, how did you—? No, never mind about that," she said, as I tried to offer an explanation. Suspended next to me, she deftly hitched me to the rope and, satisfied that the knots would hold, whistled through her teeth. The twins began hoisting me up.

My progress halted suddenly. For some agonizing instants, my heart sank. I feared something had gone amiss above us, with Vesper still in a highly precarious situation. Then I was drawn aloft even faster than before.

The twins took hold of my arms and heaved me onto the trail. I had no time to wonder how Smiler and Slider had been able to do this and still control the rope.

That same moment, I stared, astonished, at the blue-veiled face of An-Jalil.

Wasting no breath in greeting me, the noble Tawarik turned his attention and strength to hauling up Vesper. Her head and shoulders soon appeared over the edge of the cliff. At sight of him, she smiled warmly.

"I'm glad to see you, An-Jalil," she remarked, climbing to her feet and shrugging out of the rope harness. "Thank you—again."

"A bit of good luck Mr. An-Jalil happened along," said Smiler. "Slider and I had our hands full, getting the two of you back aboard and trying to keep the animals in order."

"Luck?" Vesper raised an eyebrow. "I suppose people do just happen to run into each other. Especially in the middle of the Haggar."

"Like a jinn, when needed I am there." Though An-Jalil's face was covered, I would have guessed he was smiling. Or perhaps not.

"That jinn seems to have been watching us ever since Mokarra," replied Vesper.

"I had certain business there. I was ready to leave the city when I saw you in the square, saving a poor vagabond's life. I saw courage and compassion shining like jewels. What woman is this? I wondered. Our paths matched; it pleased me to observe you. And so have I done."

"I'm glad," said Vesper. "We're in trouble with Sheik Addi. We sort of helped his daughter to elope. We need that jinn right now. Full time."

"So be it." An-Jalil nodded and indicated that we should mount and continue on our way, which I was happy to do, as I still listened uneasily for the sound of Addi's riders.

An-Jalil beckoned and his own camel obediently approached. If there is an aristocracy of these creatures, this one ranked among the noblest: Pure white, with slender legs and narrow body, it was a *mehari,* bred for speed.

"A racing camel?" Vesper gave an admiring cry.

"The swiftest of its kind. Will you ride with me, *anisah*?" An-Jalil made only the slightest gesture. The beast folded its legs gracefully—for a camel—and lowered itself to the ground. Vesper eagerly climbed aboard while An-Jalil inspected the rest of our caravan.

He was, I must say, even more skillful than Maleesh. Without so much as a word from him, the animals turned quite docile. An-Jalil assured me they would follow his own mount. My services as a camel driver were not required.

We made excellent progress. A little before sundown, An-Jalil signaled a halt where the trail widened, and he announced that we would pass the night here. Slider and

Smiler would have pitched our tents, but An-Jalil advised against it. Should we be obliged to move quickly, he did not want to abandon equipment we might need later.

"About that equipment and all the animals," said Vesper, "we were told they were a gift from Bou-Makari. I had to wonder if it was his own idea."

"My suggestion, which he wisely followed," said An-Jalil, "though I could have wished you had not used that gift to persist in your journey."

"That's something else I'd like to know," said Vesper. "Why did you warn us against Bel-Saaba?"

"Because there is a new *kahia,* a governor, in the city. Ziri el-Khouf, a man of ignorance and cruelty."

"All we want to do is give back a library book." said Vesper. "I'm sure he won't bother us on that account."

"He is a brutal man, and a dangerous one."

"We'll leave as soon as the book's safely where it belongs," said Vesper. "Besides," she added, "we'll have our jinn with us."

"Alas, no."

"But—I thought you were going to stay with us now."

"So I am," said An-Jalil, "but only to the city gates. There I shall await you."

"Not go in?" Vesper frowned. "Why? You know your way around there, which we don't."

"I am as much a stranger as you are," said An-Jalil. "The Tawarik have not set foot in Bel-Saaba for seven hundred years, nor shall we ever do so."

"I don't understand—"

An-Jalil motioned her to silence. He turned away,

head bent, listening. For a good long while he sat still, hardly breathing.

Then, in a flash, he was on his feet, holding his musket as easily as a pistol in one hand, his sword in the other.

13

Vesper followed as An-Jalil strode to the middle of the trail. By now, I clearly heard the galloping hoofbeats which the Tawarik detected sooner than even the keen-eared Vesper. The twins had jumped to their feet, and we hurried to make a stand against our pursuers.

An enormous full moon had risen, dazzlingly bright. An-Jalil made no attempt to conceal himself, only waited poised in clear view. While the sight of this blue warrior would have been enough to give any attacker second thoughts, the moonlight very likely saved the lives of the approaching riders. An-Jalil, muscles coiled like a tiger about to spring, could well have acted first and asked questions later, but Vesper called out and ran ahead.

"Maleesh! Jenna!" She embraced them as they dismounted. An-Jalil sheathed his sword and slung his musket over his shoulder. Arms folded, he silently contemplated this reunion from behind his blue veil.

"Well, sir," observed Slider, "it looks like the runaways have run back."

"We might all consider a little running," said Smiler. "That Mr. An-Jalil is some piece of work, ready to take on the whole pack of those Beni fellows. Straight out fearless. But Slider and I know a little about being outnumbered. Fearless don't answer; running does."

Whatever Vesper's opinion, at the moment she was overjoyed at the return of Maleesh and Jenna. For their part, the eloping couple looked more alarmed than delighted.

"We did not intend to rejoin you," Jenna said. "We believed you well ahead of us. We do not wish to endanger you but will keep on our separate way."

"No, you won't," returned Vesper. "I shouldn't have let you go in the first place. But—weren't you heading for Mokarra?"

"Yes," put in Maleesh. "We tried our best to avoid Sheik Addi and his band, but they saw and pursued us, forcing us south again."

Vesper turned to An-Jalil. "The tribes respect you. Take Maleesh and Jenna under your protection. Speak up for them. Sheik Addi will listen to you."

"I cannot," replied An-Jalil. "*Anisah,* understand this. It is a quarrel within families, between a father and his daughter, between a Beni-Brahim and a Beni-Hareet. To interfere would go against all custom. It would be dishonorable for me to side with one or the other in such a matter. Even if I could persuade Sheik Addi to let the couple go their way, I would be disgraced in the eyes of my own people by doing so."

"He speaks truth," Maleesh broke in, with a reverent salaam to An-Jalil. "He cannot help us, nor can you. So it is written."

"We'll see about that," said Vesper. "What we can do is get off this trail and find another. Let's have a look at Colonel Marelle's map."

Smiler produced it from his pocket. I struck a match while Vesper unfolded and studied the map closely. At last, she shook her head.

"Too bad. The only trail is the one we're on."

An-Jalil, having observed her in silence, now came and took the map from her hands.

"Have strangers drawn a picture of my homeland?" He tossed Marelle's chart to the ground. "The scribbles of a child. This shows nothing of the true Haggar. There is another trail. Only the Tawarik know it."

"Why didn't you say so right off?" returned Vesper. "We'll take that one, if you'll show us."

"The Tawarik alone have courage to follow it," An-Jalil said. "None other dares to venture there. The perils are great, *anisah.* To the body; even more, to the spirit."

"If it gets us out of here—" Vesper broke off and turned to Maleesh and Jenna. "I'm not the only one to decide. If you don't want to risk it, we'll think of something else. No matter what, I'm not leaving you two by yourselves again."

Maleesh and Jenna exchanged quick glances. Maleesh nodded. "Wherever you go, *anisah,* we shall be with you."

"So be it." An-Jalil threw back his head and gave a peculiar, vibrant call. Vesper was as puzzled as I, having no idea what the fellow was up to. A few moments later, I caught my breath in astonishment.

From the upper ledges and outcroppings, a dozen ghostly shapes sprang up, moving swiftly and noiselessly. Silver blue in the moonlight, garbed and veiled like An-

Jalil, the sight of them descending on us, leading their *meharis,* was impressive—and more than a little unnerving.

"For myself, I prefer solitude," said An-Jalil, "but my people would not have me journey unprotected. These are my close companions. They have watched over me as I have watched over you."

"Very wise of them not to let you travel alone," said Vesper, "and a good thing for us."

One by one, his warriors strode up and salaamed to their chieftain.

"Tashfin Ag Tashfin . . . Attia el-Hakk . . ." After An-Jalil presented each in turn to us, he drew apart to speak with them. Some moments later, he came back.

"I have explained your circumstances," he told Vesper. "They will go where I lead and where you wish. Our trail will take us from the Haggar a little west of Fort Iboush. There, the desert begins. We must cross a portion of it before we can again join the caravan route. We shall be well ahead of the Beni-Brahim. The path is swift for those who dare to follow it. My companions ask only to be certain the *anisah* understands the perils of her choice."

"I'll understand them better when I see them," replied Vesper.

"So be it." An-Jalil signaled to his companions. "*Anisah,* this I vow to you: Should you lose your life, it will be only if I lose mine."

I did not find much comfort in this chivalrous generosity.

Vesper smiled. "Better just make sure we all stay alive."

An-Jalil allowed us only a brief rest before setting out again. Once we started on the secret trail, Sheik Addi would not be able to follow us. The risk was his overtaking us before we reached it. To move faster and to be less heavily burdened, An-Jalil ordered us to discard about half our baggage. Also, at his instructions, we set loose our horses and mules, henceforth relying on our camels.

On the way, as if he had sniffed it out, An-Jalil halted at a shallow stream amid the rocks. We let our animals drink and filled our waterskins to the brim. At sunrise, we turned eastward and left the caravan route.

Vesper had expected our new path would take us higher among the crags. Instead, we struggled down through a rocky defile until it seemed we were at the very bottom of the Haggar; even then, the ground continued to fall sharply away. What would first appear to be a flat stretch of land strewn about with hunchbacked boulders and tall rock formations, standing alone like so many grotesque statues, often ended abruptly at the edge of a cliff.

"This must be what the moon's like," observed Vesper, scanning graveled terrain pockmarked with craters and shallow basins. The dear girl had exactly summed it up. Since, of course, it is impossible for mankind ever to set foot on that distant satellite, the Haggar is the closest equivalent, and equally desolate.

As for the perils to the body, of which An-Jalil had warned, they were what might be expected by anyone so foolish as to undertake such a journey: broken limbs, fatal falls, bruises, gashes, and all such usual inconveniences. Happily, we escaped them, thanks to An-Jalil and his companions. A stranger would never have survived, but the Tawarik could have made their way blindfolded.

Veiled as they were, it was impossible to guess the expressions on the faces of our blue guardians. I suspected they looked on the expedition as little more than a ramble in the country. They were big, rawboned warriors; the one called Tashfin stood even taller than An-Jalil. Many, in addition to their other weapons, carried barbed lances easily nine feet long and round leather shields slung at their backs. All in all, they made Colonel Marelle's Legionnaires look like a Sunday school class.

An-Jalil drove us mercilessly, taxing even Vesper's abundant vitality and stamina. The dear girl's face showed deep lines of strain, her features sunburnt and blistered, her skin cracked. Nevertheless, she set her jaw firmly, gritted her teeth, and never voiced a word of complaint. Nor, for that matter, did the twins.

"We've taken the occasional stroll through the Rockies," Slider remarked. "These Haggars are a little different, but we can't say they're much worse."

What was worse, however, were not the perils to the body but, as An-Jalil also had forewarned, the perils to the spirit. These we did not escape.

It would be fanciful to endow inanimate stones with a living personality. Yet, this lunar landscape seemed to exude an active malevolence. The sheer desolation bored into our brains and tore at our hearts. Often, during one of our brief halts, I would endeavor to nap for a few moments, only to be plagued by horrid nightmares, and would awaken crying aloud.

Vesper's eyes had taken on a glazed cast, but she fought with all her strength against the oppressiveness.

Only once did she come close to discouragement, as she turned her scorched face to me and, in a low voice, admitted, "Maybe we should have stayed in Philadelphia. You were right, Brinnie. We're going to a lot of trouble to return a library book."

Maleesh bore up as well as any of us and perhaps better. The one who suffered most was Jenna. Though she staunchly kept pace, from time to time she shuddered convulsively and her steps faltered. What sustained her were the fond ministrations of Maleesh and An-Jalil's assurances that we would soon come to the end of our ordeal.

By now, we had lost all track of time; for we did not always stop to sleep at nightfall, when the air turned bitter cold, but often continued in the icy moonlight. During the day, we stretched out for a few hours in the shade of some tormented rock formation, too exhausted to speak. The camels merely glanced at us with smug contempt.

On the morning of what An-Jalil expected to be our last full day on the trail, we set out along a rocky shelf, going on foot lest our camels lose their balance and plunge us into the ravine below.

Vesper had been keeping a sharp eye on Jenna, whose face had gone ashen, and whose gait had grown more and more unsteady. Before Vesper could reach her, the girl stumbled and sank to the ground.

14

An-Jalil motioned with his head. "See to her."

The gigantic Tashfin Ag Tashfin strode up, but Maleesh had already taken Jenna in his arms. The Tawarik chuckled at his efforts.

"Give over, little man. I can carry a burden twice that."

"No doubt," Maleesh grunted, "but she is no burden at all."

"Step back, Tashfin," An-Jalil ordered. "Let him do. If he can."

Maleesh, in fact, bore Jenna on his shoulders until we reached level ground and An-Jalil mercifully called a halt. Under the care of Vesper and Maleesh, Jenna revived. An-Jalil ordered an extra share of food and water for her.

Then he rounded on Maleesh.

"You did a foolish thing."

"I am not a wise man," replied Maleesh.

"Do you think you showed bravery?"

"No," replied Maleesh. "I am not a brave man."

"Why, then?" demanded An-Jalil.

Maleesh looked squarely at him. "It was my will to do so."

I would not have been surprised if An-Jalil had struck Maleesh for this impertinence, but the *amenokal* only turned a hard, measuring glance on him, then went to speak among his companions.

Later, An-Jalil called us all together. He announced that, by his calculations, we were at least a day ahead of Sheik Addi and his band; no question, we had safely outdistanced them. Once we reached the Sahkra, it would be only a matter of hours to Bel-Saaba. Therefore he allowed us an unexpected luxury: a full night's sleep.

Then he did something even more unexpected.

"Only among trusted friends," he said, his eyes going to each of us, "only among those we respect and love—"

He undid the portion of the turban covering his face.

"Then do we go unveiled."

He let the cloth fall aside.

An-Jalil had called himself a jinn, but I saw him as no unearthly spirit—unless the spirit of the desert itself. His cheeks and brow were pitted and grooved as if by countless sandstorms. Though his black beard was silver-shot, it gave no clue to his age. He could have been young; he could have been ancient. His mouth had the half smile of a dreamer; his eyes held the mystery of vast distances beyond any horizon. I also remembered how quick he was with a dagger.

Vesper went toward him. "For us," she said, "among those we respect and love—"

She embraced him, and we followed her example. An-Jalil's companions now put aside their blue face coverings and came to offer us their salaams. They were unnerving enough with their veils in place; without them, even more. All of them bore an assortment of scars; the huge Tashfin boasted a dozen. Attia el-Hakk had a set of teeth a wolf would have envied. Had it not been for the honor bestowed on us, I would have felt more comfortable if they had stayed masked.

Vesper, however, was soon laughing and talking among them as easily as she had done with the Legionnaires. Smiler and Slider came in for their share of admiration. The twins, indeed, seemed quite at home, as if they had been on familiar terms with this sort of rough company elsewhere. So, all in all, it was something of a festive occasion—if anything can be festive in the ghastly Haggar.

With Jenna well recovered and all of us in good spirits, we set off again at dawn the next day.

"Jenna and I shall be safe in Bel-Saaba," declared Maleesh. "Let Sheik Addi pursue us even into the city. There will be a thousand places we can hide past finding."

"Then what?" asked Vesper.

"Whatever is written," said Maleesh, "so it shall be."

It seemed to me that dancing on his hands and pulling coins from his nose was a poor profession for a married man. But I let that question go by. This was not the moment to discuss Maleesh's career opportunities.

By mid-morning, we passed through the shadows of a high-walled canyon. Emerging, the sudden flood of light nearly blinded us. Vesper shaded her eyes and scanned the barren expanse, the trembling horizon, the depthless blue of a frighteningly empty sky.

"My true home," said An-Jalil. "As el-Barak writes,

'The desert is the only purity, each grain of sand a burning truth.' Does it please you, *anisah*?"

"Yes," replied Vesper, "and compared with the Haggar, it looks downright cheerful."

I would not have applied that term. The terrain was gritty as well as hot enough to shrivel a salamander. However, we did move along with surprising speed. The course An-Jalil followed was more shale and gravel than deep sand, and he navigated skillfully between the dunes on either side of us.

We made such rapid progress that he treated us to a halt at the most miraculous phenomenon: an oasis, an island of green trees and shrubbery and tall grasses, with a diamond-clear pool of water. The camels drank; we filled our water bags, soaked our heads, and reveled in the sheer luxury of coolness.

Vesper leaned back against a palm tree, stretched out her long legs, and contemplated the surrounding expanse of sand. To all appearances, she might have been enjoying a relaxing day in Atlantic City. The dear girl, however, seldom loses the thread of a thought once it is in her mind, and now, with An-Jalil beside her on the soft grass, she returned to a question unanswered when their previous conversation had been interrupted.

"What were you telling me about Bel-Saaba?" she asked. "You said the Tawarik hadn't set foot in it for centuries. Is it forbidden to you?"

"We have forbidden it to ourselves," An-Jalil said. "Did you not know? The Tawarik founded Bel-Saaba, built the great library, planted gardens, raised fountains. It was to be a place of joy for body and mind, a happy city unmatched by any in Jedera. It thrived and prospered beyond imagination. We left it to its fate, swearing an oath from generation after generation never to return."

"I don't understand," said Vesper. "The city was thriving—so you left?"

"The blessing of prosperity brought the curse of greed," An-Jalil replied. "Bel-Saaba thrived too well. Those who came to dwell there cared little for the hopes of others and much for their own gain. Bel-Saaba grew rich—in selfishness. And blind to all but the garnering of wealth. In time, the fruit we had nurtured became rotten. We turned to the harsh purity of the desert."

"If the Tawarik governed the city," Vesper said, "couldn't they have done something about it?"

"Who can rule the passions? No law can order the spirit for good or ill. Our governors were honorable, but they failed. In those days, the office of *kahia* passed down through the eldest son of the eldest sister. After we departed, those who took power did so by force of arms, by treachery or bribery. Bel-Saaba flourished only in corruption."

I would have pointed out the difference between that shocking state of affairs and the unswerving honesty of Philadelphia's electoral processes, but Vesper interrupted.

"If it's a hereditary office," she said, "isn't there a descendant among the Tawarik today? Hasn't he ever wanted to go back, to be the *kahia* again?"

"An empty title," replied An-Jalil. "Yes, there is one among us to whom it belongs." He smiled ironically. "It is I."

❧ 15 ❧

"You're the hereditary governor of Bel-Saaba?" Vesper exclaimed. "If you wanted, you could claim your birthright—"

"Never," An-Jalil broke in. "Never shall I claim rule of a city my ancestors left to its fate. To break my vow would dishonor me."

"None of my business, of course," Vesper said, which usually means she is thinking of making it so. "It just seems to me there's more honor in trying to improve something than staying clear of it."

She would have gone on, but An-Jalil climbed to his feet and strode off, ordering his companions to remount. As we departed the oasis, his face was hard-set and remote. Vesper deemed it wise not to raise the subject again.

Soon after, we came in view of the city An-Jalil despised. For all his low opinion, Bel-Saaba was far from unattractive. It was, indeed, impressive. Set commandingly on a high plateau rising sharply from the desert floor, its walls, unlike the pink masonry of Mokarra, were golden. Or once had been. Now they were wind-ravaged and faded to a pale yellow. All around the city was the welcome sight of brilliant greenery. Thickets of palm and mimosa sprang up a little distance from the walls, along with a number of cuplike hollows, natural reservoirs of water set about with tall grass and shrubbery.

Vesper had expected An-Jalil to accompany us to Bel-Saaba's north gate, but he halted at the edge of one of the hollows. Not only had he vowed never to set foot in the city, he evidently also found it distasteful to draw closer.

His camel knelt and he dismounted. "Here, *anisah,* I take leave of you."

"But—you aren't just going to pack up and disappear?" Vesper replied. "I was hoping, after we returned the book—"

"When your task is done and you leave the city," said An-Jalil, "I will find you."

"I don't know how long we'll be," said Vesper. "We've come so far that I wouldn't want to miss a chance to look around the library."

"As you wish, but stay no longer than you must." He gave Vesper a courtly salaam. "Go in peace. Return in peace."

Ordinarily, Vesper could happily have spent several weeks exploring the fabulous library, and so could I. The warning tone in An-Jalil's voice took the edge off my appetite for extensive browsing. This apprehension grew stronger as Vesper, with Maleesh, Jenna, and the twins following, led our camels to the open gate.

There, two guardians halted us. A scruffy pair, in stained tunics and headcloths, their appearance as members of the local constabulary did not inspire great confidence. Also, instead of the muskets the Tawarik bore, they carried the latest model French rifles at their shoulders. I cannot claim they singled us out for special attention; they no doubt behaved disagreeably with all newcomers.

"We have business at the library," Vesper declared in answer to their gruff question.

One of them spat through his teeth. What he said made my heart plunge.

"Closed."

Vesper always takes an optimistic view. "You mean," she said, "it's closed for the day? When does it open again?"

The guard shook his head. "It does not."

"When they know what we're here for," said Vesper, "they'll want to open. It's important. We've come a long way—"

"Tell it to the *kahia*."

"We will," declared Vesper. "How do we find him?"

"He finds you."

We could expect no more satisfaction from this oaf. My handing over a fistful of coins only bought the vague promise that our arrival would be made known. For an added sum, the fellow grudgingly pointed the way to what I hoped would be a decent *serai*.

The lodgings were almost comfortable, probably the best available, given the atmosphere of the city. Unlike Mokarra, here I sensed no exuberance. Crowds, yes, but by and large a glum, tight-lipped lot.

"Most of them look scared to death," observed Vesper, "and the rest as if they didn't want to be here in the first place. What's the trouble?"

"Let me go to the bazaar," Maleesh suggested while the twins saw to our camels and Jenna set about arranging our quarters. "A few tricks, a little talk here and there, and I can learn more in an hour than you could discover in a week."

"Do it," said Vesper. "Brinnie and I will take a walk around, too. I won't sit cooling my heels until the governor decides to find us."

This happened sooner than expected. My donation to the guard actually produced a result. Before we could set out on our own exploration, there arrived an officious fellow with all the overbearing arrogance of a junior bean-counter.

Satisfied that we were who we claimed to be, he declared that his master, the highly exalted Ziri el-Khouf, deigned to receive us. Giving no answer to Vesper's questions regarding the library and its closing, he led us a little way from the square—where Maleesh was doubtless pulling coins out of his nose and gossip from local tongues—to Bel-Saaba's equivalent of the town hall. The terraced gardens were ill-tended and weedy, but the building itself was still quite handsome, with its arcades of pointed arches and a watchtower at one end.

The functionary ushered us into a large, airy chamber lined with graceful columns. El-Khouf, squatting on a pile of cushions, glanced up and beckoned. In front of him was a tray of melon rinds and half-eaten fruits.

Vesper never makes the mistake of judging an individual by outward appearance, knowing that the roughest exterior may conceal a heart of gold. I have tried to do likewise. In this case, however, I suspected the *kahia*'s external and internal qualities were identical. He was heavyskulled, heavy-handed, with animal cunning glinting in his beady eyes. For a chief magistrate, he was not even neat in his apparel.

This unpleasant impression of el-Khouf was not what brought us up short.

Beside the *kahia*, a rancid smile dripping over his face, stood the loathsome camel trader, the scoundrel who had sought to auction us off in Tizi Bekir: Bou-Makari.

16

Vesper is rarely at a loss for the appropriate comment. "Thanks for the camels," she said.

"Now you have brought them back to me." Bou-Makari smirked. "And yourselves, as well."

"No," said Vesper. "In fact, I thought the jinns got you."

Bou-Makari gave a nauseating laugh. "The Tawarik who cheated me had no stomach to slay an unarmed man. He forced me to compensate you and ordered me to leave Tizi Bekir. I gladly obliged, for I planned to do so in any case."

Bearing a trivial grudge is a flaw in one's character. Yet, the recollection of Bou-Makari offering to throw me in gratis at his auction still rankled.

"Villain!" I cried. "At last, you shall be brought to justice!" I turned to el-Khouf. "Sir, I have to inform you that this creature endeavored to sell us into slavery, against the laws of Jedera and the laws of humanity itself. I need not point out your duty as chief magistrate."

"This worm has already told me all that happened."
El-Khouf glared at Bou-Makari. "The *roumis* do not concern you. Lay a finger on them and you shall pay with your head. Out! Obey your orders."

While the villainous camel trader stumbled over himself in his haste to depart, el-Khouf fixed an eye on Vesper.

"What do you want here?"

After Vesper detailed our errand, el-Khouf nodded curtly. "A valuable book, you say?" He reached out, rubbing his thumb against his fingers. "Give it here."

"I think not," said Vesper.

"How is this?" cried el-Khouf. "Bel-Saaba is in my charge. The book belongs to the city. I say what shall be done with it."

To prevent him from losing more of his skimpy supply of temper, I offered a further explanation. "Sir, Miss Holly simply means that it would be more fitting to put the volume into the hands of the library director. With receipts, documents, all in proper form; perhaps even some small official ceremony to mark the occasion."

El-Khouf cocked an eye at us. "Give it to Ahmad Baba?"

"Yes, if he's the director," said Vesper.

"He is Keeper of the Scrolls," el-Khouf replied. "What, you wish to meet him? So you shall. Now."

He climbed to his feet, kicking aside the melon rinds, and ordered us to follow him. He clapped his hands and a couple guards fell in behind us as he led us out of the chamber and down the arcade.

The library buildings—there were, in fact, several—rose from what had once been a beautifully landscaped terrace of gardens and walkways. Vesper paused a moment for the pleasure of contemplating the structures and their setting. Despite signs of long neglect, Bel-Saaba's fabled library remained one of the handsomest of its kind: long vistas of archways at ground level, balconies along its upper stories, a central dome, and slender minarets.

El-Khouf hustled us on, past the guards at the entry, to the largest area. Had this been our Library Company of Philadelphia, I would have called it "the main reading room," and it was fully as impressive as that honored institution. Except that there were no readers. El-Khouf showed as much respect as he would have for a storehouse of old newspapers.

"Better than I imagined," Vesper murmured, eyes brightening as she glanced around the spacious chamber illuminated by golden shafts of sunlight. A scent of ancient leather, parchments, and papyrus hung in the air. The floor of ornamental tiles glowed, as did the polished ranks of inlaid cabinets. High racks of pigeonholes, crammed with antique volumes, honeycombed the walls. It required no great stretch of the imagination to believe one could hear the whisperings of generations of scholars in the light breeze from the exterior arcade. The only jarring note was the presence of another pair of el-Khouf's guards, rifles at their shoulders.

"Why is the library closed?" Vesper's question went unanswered as el-Khouf ushered us through a Moorish courtyard and up a long flight of steps. Another guard moved aside as the *kahia* unbolted the door.

"Ahmad Baba!" shouted el-Khouf. "Up! Visitors!" He turned a cunning glance on Vesper. "You wished to see him. Go."

Leaving el-Khouf grinning at the doorway, Vesper hesitatingly entered what appeared to be a custodial or storage area. A couple of oil lamps provided the only glimmerings of light in a small chamber at the rear.

A fragile old man rose from a couch and came to peer at us. He wore a long white caftan and a cotton skullcap. He was gray-bearded and wrinkled, but his eyes were nevertheless sharp and quick. He regarded us calmly.

"Have I merited the pleasure of visitors?" he asked, with a tinge of wry humor. "Since I want nothing of you, logic tells me that you want something of me."

"Are you the Keeper of the Scrolls?" asked Vesper.

"I have been," he said. "Whether I still am is a metaphysical question I have not resolved."

This response puzzled me as much as the situation in which we found ourselves. Reserving her inquiries on that subject, Vesper politely introduced us.

Ahmad Baba cried out in astonishment. He put his hands on her shoulders and closely studied her features.

"Can this be so? The child of Ben-Jamin el-Holly! Yes, yes, I see the father's spirit in the daughter."

"What, you knew my father?"

"Indeed I did. And well remember him. Some of his monographs are preserved in this library." Ahmad Baba had grown quite animated, beaming at Vesper, shaking his head with pleasure and amazement. "I have read his brilliant works, but here Ben-Jamin el-Holly has created a true masterpiece of beauty—in this case, an opus of joint authorship with his beloved wife.

"A most excellent scholar," Ahmad Baba went on, "but perhaps a little absentminded. When I last saw him, I permitted him to borrow a book. What was it? Yes, a treatise on medicinal herbs. By Ibn-Sina. Handwritten on vellum, very nicely decorated—alas, I must add a small reproach to his honored memory. He did not bring it back."

"I know," said Vesper. "That's what we want to talk to you about."

"Discuss Ibn-Sina? You have come so far, to this unhappy place, on an errand of botany?" The aged Keeper of the Scrolls beckoned us into his alcove. "I am a little surprised that you are alive to do so. I would have expected el-Khouf to have put you to death without delay."

"Dr. Baba," I put in, giving him that title which he surely deserved, "the volume is long overdue, but death seems rather an extreme penalty."

"It has nothing to do with books," replied Ahmad Baba. "El-Khouf is quick to put to death any suspicious stranger, lest they threaten his mastery here. Why he permitted you to live, I do not know."

"We heard he was brutal," said Vesper. "I never thought he'd be that brutal."

"He is as ruthless toward the people of Bel-Saaba. They live in constant terror of him."

"That's dreadful," said Vesper. "Why do they put up with it? Why don't they get together and rebel? That's what I'd do."

"Alas, child, for that I blame myself."

Vesper frowned. "Why blame yourself for what el-Khouf does?"

"Because I am alive." Dr. Baba sighed ruefully. "Because I am his hostage. He imprisons me here to keep the people obedient to him."

"With all respect," I put in, "a better choice of hostage would be one in a position to fight against him, to rally the citizenry. Dr. Baba, forgive me, but—you? A peaceable scholar? You pose no threat to him."

"But I do," replied Ahmad Baba. "Allow me to be immodest, but I pose a very large threat. You see, I came here years ago to accept the honored duty of caring for this priceless collection and to pursue my own studies and meditations. The people of Bel-Saaba, I soon learned, were in sorry state. Many, both young and old, could neither read nor write. I took upon myself the duty of teaching them. Also, I possess a knowledge of medicine. Thus, I strove to enlighten their minds, to heal their bodies, to lift their hearts.

"I came to love these people, and they to love me. I was grateful for their affection. Now, I wish they had been less fond of me.

"El-Khouf, not long ago, was a mere commander of the city watchmen. I do not know how he armed himself and his ruffians, but he overthrew the old *kahia* and seized power. I was among those who raised their voices against him. The strongest of us—those best fitted to lead the struggle, as you suggested, Professor Garrett—were the first to be slain. Even then, the unrest continued.

"El-Khouf is a brute, but not an altogether stupid one. Instead of killing me and further enraging the people, he kept me alive. He knew their love for me, and knew they would do nothing to endanger my life."

Dr. Baba smiled bitterly. "As a philosopher, I should have a taste for such a perfect paradox. El-Khouf is the guarantor of my well-being, which is the last thing in the world I desire. And, much as he wishes to destroy me, he does not dare. For then he would have no further hold on the people. I cannot solve the dilemma."

"We can try to help," said Vesper, who had been listening sympathetically to Dr. Baba's unhappy account. "We have good friends with us. And some others close by."

The dear girl is always quick to put her courage and intelligence to the service of justice. Sometimes, I might wish her to be less hasty in doing so. But this case, the plight of Dr. Baba touched me to the quick.

"Sir," I said, "we shall do our utmost to put an end to your disgraceful captivity. I find it profoundly distasteful, I would even say intolerable, to see a man of learning, a fellow academic, so ill-used."

We should, I suggested to Vesper, quickly return to our lodgings and discover some appropriate means, preferably within the law, of assisting Dr. Baba. The old scholar called after me as I strode to the door. My mind, however, was made up. We could not permit this situation to continue.

The door was locked.

No amount of pounding, not even my sternest demands for our release, brought any result.

"I had a feeling," murmured Vesper, "it wasn't going to be that easy."

17

Vesper, chin cupped in her hand, stood watching my useless efforts.

"Give it up, Brinnie," she advised. "They won't answer."

"Dear girl," I exclaimed, "do you not understand? We are prisoners here!"

"I understand that very well," said Vesper. "What I don't understand is, why?"

The reason for our captivity struck me as unimportant. What we had to deal with was the immediate fact. We had been locked up by an insensitive brute who did not wish us well. We had been in worse situations, but a bolted door and subsequent deprivation of liberty has always disheartened me. Vesper, however, maintained her usual calm.

"If there's a way in," she said, "there's a way out. It's just a question of finding it."

Dr. Baba had joined us meantime. Once realizing that el-Khouf had imprisoned us, the old scholar was far more distressed by our plight than Vesper, and more concerned for us than for himself.

"I do not know el-Khouf's purposes, but I am certain your lives are in peril. Ah, child, I wish you and Professor Garrett had never come to Bel-Saaba."

"We had to," said Vesper. " 'A sacred obligation,' as Brinnie calls it. To give you this."

From her tunic, she produced the little volume which had been the source of all our grief. My satisfaction at keeping my word of honor was minimal.

Dr. Baba, however, was delighted. His eyes brightened as he took the treatise and lovingly examined it.

"Blessings upon you!" he exclaimed. "After all these years, it comes back safely!"

"The book may be safe," I commented, "but you are not, nor are we. We must find a means of escape for all of us."

"That could take some time," replied Vesper. "I haven't had much chance to look around. From what I've seen, though, we don't have many choices."

"I fear you have none at all," said Dr. Baba. "I myself have studied every possibility."

Vesper's eyes had gone to a narrow opening close to the ceiling of Dr. Baba's alcove. It was hardly more than an air vent, not large enough for any of us to squeeze through.

"What about that?" Vesper went to stand on tiptoe, studying the vent. "Can we knock down the masonry around it?"

"To no purpose," said Dr. Baba. "We are too high to jump down safely. We would have to climb upward and make our way across the rooftops of the library. I am a feeble old scholar, not an acrobat. If you have the strength, make the attempt. I shall stay behind."

"I don't want to leave you," Vesper said. "I'll have to figure out something better. Now—Dr. Baba, do they keep you here all the time? Never anywhere else?"

"From time to time," said the aged librarian, "I am allowed to walk a little on the front balcony. Thus, el-Khouf shows the people of Bel-Saaba that I am still alive. I am always closely guarded on those rare occasions."

"That's useful to know," said Vesper. "It might give us some kind of chance. But I'm still trying to understand what el-Khouf has against us. It's not just a matter of getting out," she added, "it's what to do afterwards. I'm hoping An-Jalil can help us, too."

"The chieftain of the Tawarik?" Dr. Baba raised his tufted eyebrows.

"Yes," Vesper said. "He's also the hereditary governor of Bel-Saaba. Centuries ago, the Tawarik used to govern here."

"I know their history," said Dr. Baba. "I cannot blame them for abandoning the city. They are a people of noble spirit and high ideals. By their lights, they were correct in choosing the desert and the mountains. Yet, I believe they were wrong in staying aloof for these hundreds of years.

"The people of Bel-Saaba have greatly changed during that time," Dr. Baba went on. "They have been victims of one harsh governor after another, downtrodden, brutalized. El-Khouf is merely the newest. For example, in the fourteenth century—"

Dr. Baba showed every sign of beginning a long dis-

103

course. As tactfully as possible, I suggested that events of five hundred years ago could scarcely help us now.

"Alas, they cannot, Professor Garrett," Dr. Baba agreed. "Forgive me if my thoughts wander. I only intended to say that the people of Bel-Saaba would gladly welcome the Tawarik. If el-Khouf were overthrown, I have no doubt they would hail the chieftain as their rightful governor."

"I don't think An-Jalil wants to be hailed," said Vesper. "He's sworn an oath never to return to Bel-Saaba."

"Nor will he," said Dr. Baba. "He would rather die than break a vow. Indeed, he and his Tawarik must be admired for that. And yet," he added, smiling wryly, "their idealism, their inflexible honor—these are qualities ill-matched to accept the frailties of ordinary mortals. Would the citizens of Bel-Saaba be truly happy under such a rule? Would the Tawarik be happy ruling them? I do not know. But how is it that you came to encounter the chieftain himself?"

No sooner had Vesper begun her account of our treatment by the nauseating camel trader than Ahmad Baba broke in with a cry of outrage.

"Bou-Makari?" The scholar's kindly expression changed, his eyes blazed. "He is a creature of el-Khouf. He aids him in the most despicable of commerce: the slave traffic.

"I spoke of the fourteenth century," Dr. Baba went on. "In those days, Bel-Saaba was the center of that ignoble trade. For generations, the sale of slaves, of wretched beings shipped to all corners of the world, was a source of wealth—for those who conducted the reprehensible business. Over time, the slave trade dwindled. The slavers turned their attention to the western coast. Many of these were your own countrymen. Bel-Saaba no longer gained wealth from the sale of human flesh.

"In recent months, however," added Dr. Baba, "I have heard rumors of the slave traffic beginning again, under el-Khouf and his hireling."

"So we were still merchandise as far as Bou-Makari was concerned." said Vesper. "But then why did el-Khouf tell Bou-Makari to keep his hands off us, we were none of his business?"

"I understand your plight no more than you do." Dr. Baba shook his head. "Whatever the reason, it bodes ill for you."

Vesper said no more, but I knew her penetrating intellect was continuing to seek the purpose of our captivity.

"I don't suppose there's a little something to eat?" she said.

Dr. Baba begged our pardon for not having offered us refreshment. He was, as he showed us, modestly but not uncomfortably provisioned with a charcoal brazier on which he could brew mint tea, a sack of fruits, and flaps of Jederan flatbread.

"El-Khouf does not wish me to starve," he explained. "At first, I refused nourishment, hoping that would hasten my demise. His guards fed me by force—most unpleasantly. And so I gave up that futile attempt. Come, take what you wish."

Vesper gratefully accepted the old scholar's invitation. I had neither heart nor stomach to do so. While the dear girl munched away, chatting with Dr. Baba as if neither of them had a care in the world, I sank into thoughts of my faraway Mary and the unfortunate consequences of making rash promises.

Night had fallen by this time, and the only illumination came from the guttering oil lamp. A breeze had risen, hissing and whistling through the vent.

In my state of gloom, my imagination seemed to give a voice to the draft.

"Anisah! Anisah!"

I hurried to the vent, for a voice indeed it was. Vesper and Dr. Baba followed me. I distinguished a pair of eyes and a nose—upside down.

"Maleesh!" Vesper gave a glad cry. "I was sure you'd find us. How did you know el-Khouf locked us up?"

"The whole city knows," whispered Maleesh. His reversed posture, I realized, resulted from his lying prone on the roof tiles and hanging head down. "El-Khouf had it cried throughout Bel-Saaba. Two spies of the French had been captured. Once I heard that, it was only a matter of reaching you. It took longer than I expected. The guards are everywhere."

"Are the twins and Jenna all right?" asked Vesper.

"Safe," replied Maleesh. "In the bazaar, I made friends with some of el-Khouf's enemies. The twin moons and my pearl of the universe have gone into hiding with them."

"You are a friend of this brave child and the professor?" Dr. Baba put in. "You must act quickly. Remove them from here. Their lives are in utmost danger."

"I shall inform the twin moons, *anisah,*" said Maleesh. "Whatever it requires, we shall discover a means to free you. I shall return in an hour, two at most."

"Get word to An-Jalil," Vesper began.

Maleesh, however, had disappeared and was, no doubt, making his way across the tiles. He had vanished in the nick of time before a handful of el-Khouf's henchmen came stamping into Dr. Baba's chambers. Their leader gruffly announced that his chief demanded our immediate presence.

Dr. Baba was brave despite his years. He had nothing to lose but his life, and would gladly have given it up then and there. As the guards laid hold of us, he tried to fling himself on them, daring them to shoot him. The ruffians merely guffawed at his feeble efforts. They locked him up again and marched us down the steps and through the courtyard. They hustled us to the residential wing of the building and there prodded us into an apartment far more sumptuous than the governor's business office.

The chamber was hung about with beaded curtains, rich carpets covered the floor, and the heavy, spicy fragrance of incense wafted from iron braziers. At one end of the room, a pair of serving women washed and perfumed the feet of the reclining occupant of a cushioned divan.

The feet did not belong to el-Khouf.

"Do partake of some fruit, Miss Holly and Professor Garrett. I recommend the figs. They are excellent," said Dr. Helvitius.

CHAPTER

18

"We've had dinner," said Vesper.

The dear girl's face had gone pale; yet, apart from that momentary indication of shock, she stood undaunted, her glance unwavering. For my part, I confess it was all I could do to remain on my feet. My legs felt about to buckle under me, and they might well have done had it not been for Vesper's gentle but reassuring hand on my arm.

Villainy comes in a variety of degrees. Bou-Makari, for example, was an oily, treacherous, greedy creature but, no doubt, at heart a sniveling coward; the ham-fisted, thick-skulled el-Khouf, no more than a crude butcher. Despicable as they were, neither approached the towering villainy of Dr. Desmond Helvitius.

This monster, this self-styled connoisseur of art and music, this archfiend who arrogantly considered himself a member of the academic profession, surpassed that pair of common scoundrels in depth and height of undiluted infamy. No wickedness was beyond him, no maliciousness beneath him. Not long before, in the Grand Duchy of Drackenberg, he had sought to murder us, including my dear, gentle Mary, through the device of an exploding sausage. Even overlooking his previous attempts to destroy us with dynamite bombs, living burial, Gatling guns, and the cruelest of mental tortures, that lethal sausage alone put him, in my personal opinion, beyond the limits of human consideration.

"Pray reconsider, Miss Holly." Dr. Helvitius raised himself on an elbow and indicated the array of dates, oranges, figs, and pomegranates on the table beside him. He smiled cordially, revealing a set of powerful teeth. "It may be your last opportunity."

"You think so?" replied Vesper. Nevertheless, with a shrug, she accepted a handful of dates. The dear girl's analytical mind usually calculates and foresees every range of possibilities and the most unlikely turn of events. Now, she made a rare admission, "I can't say I expected to see you in Bel-Saaba."

"Surely you did not," replied Helvitius. "Yet, I expected to see you. And I am not disappointed."

He waved away the serving women who, during this exchange, had finished anointing his feet and had encased them in a pair of soft babouches. His large, muscular frame was draped in an embroidered silk shirt and voluminous pantaloons. A turban, ornamented with an egg-sized emerald, concealed his shock of white hair. He appeared much more at ease than at our last encounter, when he had made a hasty escape in a hot-air balloon.

Since then, Helvitius had obviously prospered, and prospered luxuriously. Whatever new villainy he had undertaken, he had done quite well for himself. The sight of him, smiling complacently, decked out like the Caliph of Baghdad, might cause one to question the justice of the world. Virtue, however, is its own shining reward. We, at least, could take justifiable pride in having fulfilled a sacred obligation despite our present misfortune. In pointing this out to him, I spared him none of my contempt.

"But, Professor Garrett," he replied, "you and Miss Holly both look in reasonably good condition, all things considered."

"No thanks to you," returned Vesper.

"On the contrary, it is thanks to me." Helvitius sat up on his divan. "You are alive; you have been kindly treated—compared with what el-Khouf wished to do with you. I was not here to welcome you personally, but I gave express orders that you were not to be harmed."

"You?" Vesper is seldom taken aback by events no matter how unexpected. At this, she startled and came as close to outright astonishment as I had ever seen. "You gave el-Khouf orders?"

"Naturally. He follows my instructions. As you may have observed, he is an individual of forceful actions but limited mental capacity. He is useful, in fact essential to me. His natural inclinations, however, must be curbed and properly directed."

"Oh, Brinnie," Vesper murmured in vexation and self-blame, "I should have known that lout wasn't doing all this without orders from someone else."

We both, no doubt, should have suspected. Whatever evil roamed the world, the probabilities were excellent that Helvitius had a finger in it. Even so, to imagine him in the distant reaches of Jedera stretched suspicion beyond normal limits. I urged the dear girl not to reproach herself.

Vesper faced Helvitius again. "Then I guess you're the one who told el-Khouf to denounce us as French spies. That's a lie and you know it."

"A convenient untruth," Helvitius corrected. "If the citizens of Bel-Saaba feel threatened by the French, they will pay less attention to their own situation. It was a happy opportunity."

"So now, I suppose you'll have us shot," said Vesper.

"Heavens no," replied Helvitius. "That would be a pointless waste of still another opportunity."

"Then what?" Vesper demanded.

"I intend to make good use of you," said Helvitius. "The world, Miss Holly, abounds in rich resources. It requires the eye of the imagination to recognize them.

"For example," he continued, "I first came to Bel-Saaba with an altogether different goal in mind—a goal, I should add, I am on the brink of achieving. At the same time, I found el-Khouf making energetic but disorganized attempts to establish a highly profitable enterprise."

"The slave trade," said Vesper. "Yes, that suits you."

"Have you stooped so low?" I burst out. "I thought that you had already overstepped every boundary of human decency. This infamous traffic surpasses all else."

"For which, in a sense, I thank Miss Holly," replied Helvitius. "You know my wealth is considerable, greater than you could possibly imagine. But Miss Holly's constant interference has, I confess, caused me significant financial damage. I merely wished to regain what she has made me lose. And so I shall, a thousandfold.

"The slave trade, regrettably, is illegal in many parts of the so-called civilized world. Yet, that is a blessing in disguise. The supply of slaves has decreased. Therefore the demand, and thus the price, have increased: a simple law of economics. Even in realms where slavery is accepted, or at least winked at by the authorities—Arabia, the Ottoman Empire, the Far East, to name only a few—it has become a most lucrative commerce.

"What my imagination allowed me to envision," Helvitius went on, in a tone of almost poetic fervor, "was a vast organization with its center in Bel-Saaba. An efficient, well-regulated network—which I can easily achieve through my close acquaintance with so many individuals in high places throughout the world—drawing its inventory from Ethiopians, Circassians, Turkomans, and other benighted peoples, to meet the demands of an eager market. In short, Miss Holly, adapting the same methods as your own barons of industry."

The audacity of this archvillain in subverting the honored practices of American enterprise to the basest of transactions shocked me as much as the slave trade itself. Then the implications of his vile scheme, as they pertained to us, struck me with such horror that my head reeled.

Vesper understood the significance immediately. "You won't shoot us. You'll sell us."

"I have not yet decided," Helvitius replied. "When Bou-Makari came to Bel-Saaba and reported his misadventure, I instantly realized—to my astonishment and delight—that you and Professor Garrett were making your way here, into my waiting hands. What to do with you? The possibilities are richly varied.

"Yes, Miss Holly, I might sell you. Or make a special

gift of you to an important gentleman in Constantinople. Or Damascus. Or farther. Or even," he added pleasantly, "keep you for myself. With Professor Garrett. Or without him."

"Monster!" I cried. "Miss Holly will choose death before such dishonor, and so will I. You shall neither sell nor separate us. I shall die before I permit it."

"That is yet another possibility. I must ponder it." He set his glance on Vesper. "Much will depend on Miss Holly and her degree of cooperation."

"I can tell you the degree," Vesper said. "Zero."

"You may be less hasty in your decision when you see what else I offer," said Helvitius.

"You needn't offer anything." Vesper made no attempt to conceal a yawn.

The dear girl, no doubt, was exhausted by this painful conversation with the abominable Helvitius. Past a certain point, even villainy grows tiresome. Then I recalled that Maleesh had promised to come to Dr. Baba's chamber within an hour or two. Surely he would have our rescue already in train. Vesper had understood that our time was too precious to waste in listening to Helvitius's threats.

"It's been a trying day," she added. "I haven't any more to say to you. You might as well lock us up again."

"So I shall." Helvitius gestured to his guards. "In due course. You are both leaving Bel-Saaba. You shall not return."

When civility, moral resolution, and all else fail, Vesper resorts to physical action. That failed as well. Despite our struggles, the guards overcame us and quickly bound us hand and foot. Vesper then employed her voice, not an altogether feeble weapon, in the vain hope that her shouts might somehow reach sympathetic ears. The only result was that gags were forced into our mouths.

At first, I hoped that Maleesh might eventually locate our new place of imprisonment. My heart sank when I realized we were being removed from Bel-Saaba then and there. Flung over the backs of horses, we clattered and jolted through empty streets. The city lay deserted, undoubtedly under strict curfew.

We emerged, as best I judged, not from the north gate but the south, and struck out across the countryside. We continued some uncomfortable while until our captors slowed their pace. My position made it difficult to see where they had brought us. Under the bright moon, I could only glimpse a long, low structure, white as dry bones. What once had been towers rose at either end, so eroded by wind and sand that they appeared to be skeleton fingers twisting skyward.

We were unloaded at a side entrance, roughly hauled through a honeycomb of passages and chambers, and at last shoved into a small stone cell. Our captors, at least, had the common decency to untie us and remove our gags before bolting the massive door upon us.

"Where is this?" Vesper lost no time surveying our sparse, even monastic, quarters. There was little to survey: no sleeping accommodations, no furniture, only thick walls of white stone; and, in one, a window barred by an iron grille.

"We're close to some foothills," Vesper pointed out as I came to peer through the grille. "If I've got my bearings right, they're south of Bel-Saaba. The Hambra Mountains?"

Topography, I suggested, did not immediately concern us.

"Not right now," said Vesper, "but it might be good to know, if we can find a way out."

My heart filled with admiration. Here, even in the most hopeless circumstances, the dear girl's thoughts had turned confidently toward eventual freedom. Though I applauded Vesper's indomitable spirit, I feared it would avail us nothing. Nor would the efforts of Maleesh. We were far beyond his attempts at rescue.

Vesper turned away from the window and sniffed the air. "Notice that smell, Brinnie?"

I could hardly fail to do so. I had been aware of it when we were conducted here; with other concerns in my mind, I had disregarded it.

"In Mokarra," Vesper murmured. "On the day of the fire. I smelled it there, too. The cargo for Bel-Saaba?"

Speculation was pointless. To me, the vile odor was merely an added discomfort, for our cell was bitter cold. Vesper, arms wrapped around her, paced back and forth while I sank down on the stone floor.

"Whatever Helvitius has in mind," she said at last, as if reading my thoughts, "he's not going to separate us."

"Dear girl," I groaned, "I could bear anything but that."

"He won't, Brinnie. That much, I'm sure of."

"How can you prevent him? We are in his power. And at his mercy, of which he has none at all."

"That's the only part I'm not sure about," said Vesper.

Nevertheless, her tone of resolution and Philadelphia dignity in the face of the most shameful prospects kept me from giving way to complete despair. Then, as if noxious odors were not enough, our unhappy state was further aggravated by sounds of rattling and clanking.

"Have they got some kind of factory here?" Vesper listened carefully awhile, but could find no reasonable interpretation.

The primary effect of this racket was to deprive us of sleep. Vesper usually dozes peacefully, whatever the circumstances. Now she remained as wakeful as I. All in all, we passed a miserable night. The morning promised to be worse, the sun turning our cell into an oven.

Vesper pricked up her ears as the bolts at our door were drawn. "Breakfast?"

"Good morning." Dr. Helvitius, flanked by his rifle-bearing ruffians, stood in the doorway. He had exchanged his turban and silken garments for a jacket and pair of riding breeches. A cloth cap sat jauntily atop his white hair. The scoundrel looked cheerful and well rested.

"I spoke to you of my original purpose in coming to Bel-Saaba," he said, as we were marched down one of the narrow corridors. "It is of far more importance, and profit, than even the wealth I shall derive from my enterprise with el-Khouf.

"As you shall see, Miss Holly, it is a work of profound significance. I do not exaggerate when I assure you I will change the entire course of history."

"I'm sorry for history," muttered Vesper.

We had, by now, left the honeycomb of chambers to emerge on a flat, sun-baked expanse surrounded by the eroded walls and towers I had glimpsed the night before.

"Long ago," said Helvitius, "this place held ancient tombs. It was, as well, a place of seclusion and meditation. It suits my requirements admirably."

He clapped his hands and a ragged crew of unhappy-looking wretches pulled away the canvas tenting draped over some large object.

Vesper caught her breath. I could only stare, not believing my eyes. What I saw convinced me that Helvitius had finally overstepped the limits of sanity.

"With this," he proudly declared, "I shall reshape the destinies of every nation on earth."

❧ 19 ❧

What stood before us was an impossibility. Over the centuries, intellects more powerful than that of Helvitius had vainly striven to comprehend this baffling mystery. Swedenborg, the learned scientist and theologian; the Englishmen, Stringfellow and Henson; and so many others— all had failed, even the great Leonardo da Vinci. But Helvitius, in his overweening arrogance, gestured grandly toward this insane conglomeration.

A long rectangle of oiled fabric, stretched upon a wooden frame, surmounted a wicker cage equipped with wheels. At the rear spread a fishtail contraption with fan-like blades attached. Wires, rods, and braces held the structure together. It was not only an impossibility; it was lunacy.

"A flying machine!" exclaimed Vesper.

Helvitius beamed with insufferable pride. "I knew that you, Miss Holly, would recognize the magnitude of my achievement."

One should not take pleasure in the failure of a fellow

scholar's efforts. In the case of Helvitius, however, it served him right. I confess to a measure of satisfaction as I addressed him.

"Sir," I said, "have you brought us here to display your useless apparatus? What you call an achievement violates every law not only of science but, as well, natural philosophy. You have wasted your ill-gotten fortune in a hopeless effort. Had nature, in her wisdom, intended us to fly, she would have endowed us with the means to do so."

Helvitius disregarded my irrefutable logic, beckoning Vesper to draw closer and examine this ungainly contrivance. To my astonishment, she seemed momentarily to have forgotten our desperate situation, thoroughly intrigued by the ridiculous mechanism.

"Observe the excellence of construction," said Helvitius. "The most skilled of Bel-Saaba's metalsmiths, jewelers, and cabinetmakers have fabricated it under my instruction."

Vesper is always practical. "Yes, but does it work?"

"It will," replied Helvitius, with bland confidence. "It must. I have devoted the most intense study to every aspect of its engineering and design. I have deeply pondered the works of Archimedes, Roger Bacon, and the latest researches by the Swiss Bernoulli. I have understood why others have failed, and, therefore, why I shall succeed.

"I have accomplished what no previous inventor has done. I have solved the problem of combining lightness of weight with the most powerful motive force."

Helvitius directed Vesper's attention to an array of pipes, tanks, and what appeared to be a combustion chamber. "A steam engine of my own design, Miss Holly. A steam engine the like of which has never been dreamed, let alone produced. It is the most compact, powerful, and efficient of its kind.

"Its components were machined to my specifications by a dozen different manufacturers throughout Europe, so that no individual could guess the full nature of its construction."

"Nicely made," Vesper admitted, herself an excellent student of engineering, among her other numerous abilities. "One question: What makes it go?"

"A volatile liquid from your own state of Pennsylvania," replied Helvitius. "A substance heretofore discarded as worthless, yet, in fact, the world's most remarkable fuel. For lack of a better term, I call it 'petrol.' It is fractioned from a type of naphtha."

"Of course!" exclaimed Vesper. "That's what I smelled here—and in Mokarra."

"No doubt you did," said Helvitius. "I was awaiting such a cargo. Unfortunately, much of it was destroyed by fire. It is only a temporary loss. Petrol is abundant and inexpensive. I shall replace my stock with a later shipment."

Vesper cast her eyes over the contrivance, nodding to herself as if she seriously considered it might have practical application. "Why here? Bel-Saaba isn't the most convenient place in the world."

"For my purposes, it is," replied Helvitius. "Its very remoteness guards my secrecy. But there is another reason, more important—indeed, vitally essential to my work. Bel-Saaba's library.

"Previous experimenters have followed the wrong path. They have not grasped the true nature of what I might call 'aerodynamics.' One genius alone understood it, but he had not the benefit of our modern materials and techniques to put it into practice, and so it remained only a theory, overlooked and long forgotten.

"That scientific genius, whose vision reached far ahead of his time, a Moorish Leonardo da Vinci, is Souliman Ibn-Salah. His works are housed in only one place: the Bel-Saaba library.

"The writings of Ibn-Salah are the key to all my efforts. From this ancient genius, I have gleaned the secret which no human being in our modern age has grasped: the secret of flight. You see it here embodied in this vehicle."

"Suppose you're wrong?" asked Vesper.

"Not I, Miss Holly. Ibn-Salah. If his theories are incorrect, then I must conclude that a flying machine is, in fact, impossible. However, I do not foresee that will be the case."

"You will have conducted a pointless experiment nevertheless," I put in. "Your device can have no practical application. As a means of transporting goods and passengers, it will be no more useful than a child's kite."

Helvitius gave me an arrogant glance. "Your imagination, Professor Garrett, unlike my own, is sadly limited and earthbound. Did I speak of passengers? Of transportation? No, sir, I did not. My flying machine will carry a different cargo."

Helvitius turned his eyes upward in an expression of dreamy pleasure. "What, then, will it carry? Bombs, Professor Garrett. Powerful explosive charges."

Vesper's face paled with horror as this monstrous madman continued, "Destruction will literally rain from the air. Cities, human habitations, bridges, railroads, whole armies in the field—none can escape. Every nation will beg to purchase my invention. They must. At any price. For I am the sole supplier, the sole possessor of the secret of its manufacture. If I sell a fleet of my machines to France, Germany must likewise buy them. So must Great Britain, and your own United States.

"Dare you tell me now, Miss Holly, that I exaggerated when I said my work would change the course of history? It will change the entire nature of warfare, an occupation which has constituted so much of our civilization."

Vesper said nothing for some moments; nor could I find words for any adequate response to this most diabolical of all his villainous schemes.

"Leave it to you to think of something like that," Vesper at last replied. "Still—how do you know it will work?"

"I do not know," said Helvitius. "My invention has yet to be tried aloft, and Ibn-Salah's theories demonstrated not in the pages of a book but in the skies."

"With any kind of luck," said Vesper, "you might break your neck."

Helvitius laughed in high good humor. "Do you think me so foolhardy? Surely, you have learned to know me better in the course of our acquaintance. No, no, the risks at this early stage are far too great. Endanger myself? Not in the least.

"You, Miss Holly, shall be the first to test my flying machine."

CHAPTER

❧ 20 ❧

"Reptile! Miscreant!" Scarcely able to control my outrage, I shook a fist at the smiling fiend. "You are condemning her to death!"

"Steady on, Brinnie." Vesper laid a calming hand on mine as she replied to Helvitius, "What happens if I won't?"

Helvitius shrugged. "To me, it makes little difference. To you, a great deal. Until your opportune arrival, I had planned to instruct one of these mechanically skilled individuals"—he gestured at the workmen regarding us in unhappy silence—"in the operation of my aircraft. The controls could not be simpler. Even the most ignorant could master them. But you, Miss Holly, with your knowledge of physics, engineering, kinetics, would be better able to report any technical flaws in my design.

"If you are unwilling," he added, "I shall manage without your assistance. Before you make your final decision, I urge you to consider your alternatives. On the one hand, a life of involuntary servitude in some distant clime, far from Professor Garrett. On the other, I might allow you to remain here with me, to aid in my further research. You would find it a stimulating challenge. You might also wish to conduct your own scientific investigations. Professor Garrett would find the contents of the library sufficiently interesting to occupy his life—whose duration, of course, depends on your obedient behavior."

"A devil's bargain!" I cried. "Dear girl, pay no heed!"

Vesper, to my dismay, instead of rejecting this vile proposal out of hand, hesitated for some moments. Turning her attention to the flying machine, she said to Helvitius, "Before I decide one way or the other, I'd have to know how it works. You claim it's easy? I want to see that for myself."

Dr. Helvitius nodded, beckoning for us to approach the vehicle. He opened a hatchway in the framework. Vesper bent and crawled inside. There, with great interest, she examined the apparatus while Helvitius continued, "The controls are extremely delicate, but their manipulation is simplicity itself. The vertical rod directs the machine up or down. The pedals at your feet cause the craft to turn left or right. The small lever in front of you regulates the fuel supply and speed; the larger one, forward motion."

"It looks easy enough," said Vesper. "Let me make sure I've got it all straight. Now, what was it you told me? This stick? Oh, yes. It makes the machine go right or left."

"Not the stick, Miss Holly," Helvitius replied impatiently. "The pedals, as I have just this moment explained, control sideways motion."

"Which pedals?"

"The ones in the flooring," snapped Helvitius. "I advise you to pay closer attention."

"Oh, yes," Vesper said. "Now I see them."

She leaned down. A moment later, I heard the sound of ripping and the jangling of wires. Helvitius cried out angrily as Vesper crawled from the hatchway.

She held up a tangle of broken wires and shattered rods. Marvelous girl! With a few energetic tugs, she had destroyed what appeared to be the entire control mechanism.

"Is this what you meant?" she innocently inquired. "You're right, they're delicate."

The face of Helvitius tightened. "I take it, Miss Holly, that is your answer."

"No," said Vesper. "I'm still thinking it over. By the time you have all this repaired, I'll be ready to decide. It could take awhile, I guess, but we're in no hurry."

"Miss Holly," Helvitius said icily, "you have made a serious miscalculation."

If Vesper expected him to remand us to our cell, she had indeed miscalculated. Instead, Helvitius ordered horses to be brought. He mounted and, under the aimed rifles of the guards, we were compelled to do likewise.

"Dear girl," I whispered, as our cavalcade of guards, Helvitius leading, trotted from the courtyard, "your action was courageous. Alas, I fear it will only bring some new punishment."

"I knocked his flying machine out of kilter, anyway," said Vesper. Then she added, "I'm half sorry I did. Really, Brinnie, he'd put it together very nicely. Fascinating. I wish I'd seen more of that new engine, too."

Vesper left off as Helvitius turned his mount and came to ride next to us. Until now, I had assumed we would be taken to Bel-Saaba, there to face what further devilry the monster had in store. Once away from the eroded building, we headed not in the direction of the city but into the Hambra foothills.

"I salute your enterprise and daring, as I have come to know them so well," remarked Helvitius, "but now I give you fair warning. For your own sake, Miss Holly, give no thought to escape in these hills. As you see, my men carry the latest and most accurate rifles—which I myself obtained through, let us say, private channels. Believe me, neither you nor Professor Garrett would live long enough to enjoy even temporary freedom."

Helvitius pronounced this threat in a completely matter-of-fact tone and would, unquestionably, have carried it out in the same fashion. The prospect of being shot down in our tracks was enough to dampen Vesper's usual optimism. She lapsed into silence as we passed through the scrubby vegetation of an ascending trail.

Midday had passed before we ceased jogging upward and Helvitius led us over a relatively flat stretch to a peculiar construction created not by nature but the labor of human hands.

A long, steep slope had been cleared along a hillside. This roadway, or smooth track, swooped sharply downward, ending abruptly as it overlooked the countryside below.

Vesper gasped and clapped a hand over her mouth. Helvitius had swung from his saddle, calling out orders to a group of his enslaved laborers.

"I did miscalculate," Vesper murmured. "Brinnie, he's got another one."

A second flying machine! My heart sank as Vesper pointed to an identical craft moored with ropes at the upper end of the track.

"You should not be surprised." Helvitius came up to us and indicated that we should dismount. "What you saw before, Miss Holly, was an earlier model for purposes of study and demonstration. This newer one has been improved in many details. The system of control remains the same. You have already been instructed in its operation. I am resolved to launch my vehicle without delay.

"I shall spare you the painfulness of indecision and long-drawn-out shilly-shallying. Miss Holly, you will accept or decline this opportunity here and now. Immediately."

"If you put it that way," said Vesper, "then—yes, I'll do it."

"This is deliberate murder!" I burst out. "You give her no chance even to practice manipulating your infernal machine."

"I rely on Miss Holly's intelligence and ability," replied Helvitius. "She is resourceful, quick to learn, and these qualities will be enhanced by a strong motivation: Her life is at stake."

"So is your flying machine," said Vesper.

"I can always build another," said Helvitius. "You cannot do likewise."

"I insist on accompanying her," I declared. "You shall not allow her to face this peril alone."

"You insist?" returned Helvitius. "You are not in a

position to insist on anything. It is I who insist. Yes, Professor Garrett, you shall join her. You shall aid in her observations and make note of all significant details."

At that, he left us and went to converse with his laborers. Vesper took my arm and hurriedly whispered, "There's no other way, Brinnie. We have to take our chances." She hesitated a moment, then added, "One thing worries me, though."

"I share your apprehension," I said. "I, too, fear this monstrous apparatus will crash."

"No," said Vesper, "I'm worried that it won't. It might really fly. I'll have to make sure it doesn't."

❧ 21 ❧

"Don't you see, Brinnie? One way or another, he has to believe his machine's a failure. If he sees it really works, you know what he'll do. His slave trade's bad enough. But if every country in the world can drop bombs on each other—no, Brinnie, I won't let that happen."

"But we are risking our lives and may very well lose them."

"Not yours, Brinnie. No, your life's the one thing I won't risk. I didn't think Helvitius would make you come along. I'll talk him out of it."

"That you will not," I answered. "Whatever fate holds in store, I will share it. You cannot deny me. I will be with you."

"Dear old Brinnie," Vesper murmured. "I wouldn't want you anywhere else."

She said no more as Helvitius returned to hand us each a pair of close-fitting green spectacles and a cap equipped with a leather chin strap.

"You may find the air currents quite strong," he said,

while we donned those items. "Unlike a balloon, which sails at the mercy of the wind, my flying machine is susceptible to direction. It will go where you wish. If my calculations are correct, you should be able to remain aloft long enough to demonstrate its functions."

"And if your calculations aren't correct?" said Vesper.

"You shall discover that very quickly." Helvitius fixed a baleful eye on Vesper. "I understand your mental processes, Miss Holly. I suspect that even now you contemplate some manner of escape."

"Last thing in the world I was thinking about," said Vesper.

"How sensible," said Helvitius, "because escape is impossible. There is not enough fuel to carry you any great distance. And where, in any case, could you hide? The open desert? My men are watching below; you would be seen and recaptured easily. I, too, shall observe your every movement," he added, indicating a pair of binoculars slung over his shoulder.

Helvitius motioned for us to proceed to the upper end of the runway, where the flying machine awaited. I squeezed through the hatch and took up a cramped position at the back of the wheeled cage. Vesper climbed in after me. As she settled herself at the controls, Helvitius produced a large revolver which he pointed directly at her.

"None of your clever but ultimately futile tricks," he said coldly. "If I perceive one suspicious move on your part, I will shoot both of you instantly.

"Now, Miss Holly, I suggest you brace yourself securely. My machine, as yet, has insufficient power to lift itself from the ground. Hence, this runway will allow it to achieve maximum velocity before the moment of flight."

Helvitius paused, turning his eyes to the clouds. "As a classical scholar, I am naturally reminded of the myth of Daedalus and Icarus, with myself, of course, as Daedalus the artificer. And Icarus—Miss Holly, I sincerely hope you do not share the fate of that unfortunate youth. Do not fly, in the figurative sense, too close to the sun."

With a disgusting look of self-satisfaction at having made this unsettling allusion, Helvitius closed the hatchway. "Now, I can only wish you bon voyage."

"Bon voyage?" muttered Vesper. "Better say something like happy landings."

One of the artisans, meantime, had activated the powerful engine, which began roaring and chugging. The blades at the rear of our cage spun into motion as the crew unloosed the mooring lines.

On either side of the vehicle, the crew laid hold of the framework and pushed it down the slope, running along until the machine gained such speed that no longer could they keep up with it.

We shot over the brink. Suddenly free from the reassuring solidity of earth, we hung poised for an instant. The top of my head felt detached from the rest of me as the nose of the flying machine dipped, and the vehicle plunged downward.

"Hold on, Brinnie!" Vesper shouted above the roar of the engine. "Hold tight!"

My cry of terror seemed to hang in the air above us, along with my stomach. Vesper grasped the vertical rod and struggled to pull it toward her. We continued to plummet. The desert floor came closer at an alarming rate, until, at last, the flying machine righted itself. The wing above our enclosure shuddered as if it might rip apart under the strain. Then we swooped upward, soaring past the slopes of the Hambra. Helvitius, binoculars trained upon us, had become a tiny, insignificant figure.

I clapped my hands over my ears to shield them from the deafening whir of the blades and the racketing engine. I could scarcely catch my breath. Had human beings ever been propelled through the air at such speed? In defiance of nature's own inviolable laws? Despite the churning of my interior organs, the sensation was not altogether disagreeable.

Vesper glanced back at me, her face alight with sheer joy. "Brinnie, it's marvelous! What a shame to smash it!"

Maintaining her grip on the rod, she endeavored to operate the pedals. The flying machine gave a lurch and sheered off to starboard. The wires twanged, the wooden struts rattled as she trimmed the craft and set it straight again. The engine, meantime, had developed a sort of bronchial cough. With a sickening drop, the vehicle lost its former altitude.

"Helvitius got his calculations wrong," Vesper called back to me, "or he misunderstood Ibn-Salah. The machine isn't staying up. I won't have to crash on purpose," she added. "That's going to happen by itself. If I can catch the air currents, I'll try to fly it like a kite and think of an easy way to land."

Helvitius, for all his arrogance, had failed to defy nature. There was, at least, some small consolation in that. The engine, by now, had ceased functioning. A stench of overheated metal filled my nostrils. A geyser of steam spurted from the rear of our cabin.

We continued, nevertheless, to be airborne. Vesper's brilliant manipulation of the controls carried us in the direction of Bel-Saaba.

Vesper pointed downward. "What's burning?"

Indeed, a cloud of black smoke rose from what I could discern to be the library building. Vesper brought us farther down until we nearly skimmed the walls. The public square seethed with running figures.

"El-Khouf's guards! There—Brinnie, those people fighting in the street. They look like Addi's tribesmen!"

At that moment, a blast of heat scorched me. A backward glance told me that the fishtail assembly had caught fire.

"That's Sheik Addi himself!" exclaimed Vesper. "He's in trouble, too. The guards have him cornered.

"Hang on, Brinnie," she added. "If we have to crash, we'll do it in Bel-Saaba."

❧ 22 ❧

"No way to crash gently," Vesper called out. "I'll do what I can."

She pulled back on the guidance rod and kicked at the pedals on the flooring. The flying machine veered and dipped as Vesper fought with all her might to control this diabolical invention which, I had no doubt, would provide our final resting place. The aircraft tilted to one side then the other. We had, by now, cleared the city walls and were speeding toward the town hall at the breathtaking rate of what I judged to be some fifteen or even twenty miles an hour.

As the last remaining wires snapped, Vesper brought the yawing vehicle earthward, heading for the terraces and gardens. The ground heaved up to meet us.

Vesper kicked open the hatchway. "Jump! Now!"

She flung herself from the cage. I plunged after her, to go sprawling into a bank of shrubbery. Brave girl! Her presence of mind and calm courage had kept us from breaking our limbs and, very probably, our necks as well.

The flying machine continued on its course, skidding across the dry fountain basin while flames streaked from the fishtail. Moments later, it shattered against the trunk of a palm tree. The subsequent explosion sent blazing fragments of cloth, wood, and metal into the air.

Vesper disentangled herself from the bushes, tore off the spectacles and cap, and was running across the terrace by the time I collected my wits and stumbled to catch up with her. The immediate result of our arrival and the destruction of the flying machine was to flush out the nauseating Bou-Makari from behind the palm tree.

Whatever the events taking place in the city, the treacherous camel trader had apparently chosen to observe them from this vantage point. In view of the explosion and the debris raining down on him, the terrified Bou-Makari opted to leave the vicinity. Knees pumping, turban unwinding to stream behind him, he raced off as if the jinns themselves were at his heels.

Vesper's observations from aloft had been correct. Sheik Addi was indeed in Bel-Saaba and, at the moment, hard pressed by some of el-Khouf's guards. A further benefit of the exploding machine had been to send portions of the shattered wing spinning into the pack of ruffians besetting him. They scattered and fled, while Addi stared agape at the flaming wreckage.

"Addi!" Vesper ran up to him. "What are you doing here?"

The sheik popped his eyes at her. "We came to save you."

"We're saved already," Vesper replied. "Save the library."

The smoke which had first drawn her attention to the

city continued rising from the library building. Too bewildered to do otherwise, Sheik Addi obeyed Vesper's command, beckoning to some of the Beni-Brahim tribesmen close by, and set off across the terrace.

Vesper would have followed, but as she started up the flight of steps, Jenna ran from the arcade and seized her by the arm.

"Flee the city!" cried Jenna. "*Anisah,* make haste!"

"Where's Maleesh?" Vesper demanded. "Where are the twins?"

In reply, Jenna only continued urging Vesper to make her escape. "The north gate. Go, *anisah!* An-Jalil awaits you!"

"I'll go," said Vesper, "as soon as you tell me what's happening."

Any explanation could, in my opinion, be offered later. I took Vesper's arm and, despite her protest, pulled her away and rather forcibly directed her across the square.

We broke clear of a knot of townspeople armed with cudgels, eagerly joining the Beni-Brahim in confronting the guards.

Though Helvitius had armed el-Khouf's ruffians with the latest firearms, he had apparently given them inadequate instruction in their use. Most of their shots went wild, and, exhausting their supply of cartridges, they were compelled to employ their rifles as clubs. In the hand-to-hand melee, it was difficult to judge which side held the advantage.

The north gate stood open. We ran toward it. "There!" cried Vesper. "The Tawarik!"

That moment, a blow to the back of my head sent me

pitching to the ground. Half stunned, I staggered to my feet. What I saw caused me to shout in horror.

El-Khouf had gripped Vesper with one burly arm. With his other hand, he brandished a dagger.

"Stand away!" he ordered me. "I pass or the *roumi* dies."

"Villain!" I exclaimed. "As villainous as your master! If you dare to harm her—"

Vesper, for her part, kicked and struggled, striving to wrench herself away from el-Khouf's grasp. Little by little, her efforts brought her and her captor closer to the gate. There, I caught sight of the giant Tashfin, of Attia, and of An-Jalil himself.

"Help us!" called Vesper. "Here!"

An-Jalil understood her plight immediately. Eyes blazing above his blue veil, a terrifying war cry on his lips, he sprang through the gate, his vow shattered, the first Tawarik to set foot in Bel-Saaba for seven centuries.

Sword in hand, An-Jalil sped toward the *kahia*. "Coward! Do you hide behind a woman?"

El-Khouf bared his teeth. "Tawarik, let me pass."

"Stand against me first," declared An-Jalil. "Face me in single combat, if you dare." He raised his sword.

El-Khouf gave a scornful laugh at An-Jalil's weapon. He flung Vesper aside. Before she could regain her feet, he drew a revolver from his tunic. Vesper cried out as he fired.

An-Jalil pitched forward. The sword dropped from his hand. El-Khouf spun around and darted through the crowd. Tashfin, shouting with rage, set after him for a few paces; then, concerned more for his fallen leader, he turned back. An-Jalil's other warriors ran to help him. Vesper was there before them, kneeling at An-Jalil's side.

"Take me to the desert," he murmured. "There, it is a clean death."

CHAPTER

23

"You aren't going to die in the desert or anywhere else." Vesper drew aside his veil and loosened the collar of his tunic. Under the blue stain, An-Jalil's face was mottled gray.

"We must obey him." Tashfin knelt beside her. The huge Tawarik's eyes brimmed. "Take him from this accursed city. He told me death awaited him if he set foot within, yet he did so. Now we shall do as he commands. So it is written."

"Not yet it isn't," Vesper declared, though as near to weeping as Tashfin. "The only place we'll take him is to a doctor."

An-Jalil's eyes had closed; his breathing came in shallow gasps. The warriors gathered around him, ready to follow their chieftain's last order. Although the fray continued on the far side of the square, the Tawarik had no heart to join it. Had things fallen out differently, there was no doubt in my mind that they would have made short work of el-Khouf's ruffians. It was questionable now whether we could even make good our own escape.

"Anisah!"

Maleesh had arrived. He cried out at the sight of the fallen An-Jalil.

"We need Dr. Baba. Right away," Vesper told him. "Where is he?"

Maleesh gestured toward the library. "Perhaps he is still there. I do not know. El-Khouf's men bar the way."

Though I saw nothing of el-Khouf himself, his guards indeed had taken a position along the arcade and showed every sign of preparing to attack the tribesmen. As I judged the situation, the Beni-Brahim stood an excellent chance of being defeated. The element of surprise might, at first, have worked in their favor, but the tide of battle was now rapidly turning against them.

"Tashfin," Vesper pleaded, "go help Sheik Addi and his people. They'll be killed if you don't."

The big Tawarik glanced up in the direction of the fighting. His eyes glittered with vengeance. He nodded curtly and sprang to his feet. He motioned to Attia el-Hakk and half a dozen of the others, who unslung their muskets and set off across the square.

Vesper ordered the remaining Tawarik to carry An-Jalil to a more sheltered spot near the wall. Maleesh, during this, had not ceased urging Vesper to flee the city. To me, it was excellent advice, which Vesper determinedly ignored.

The crash of the flying machine must have damaged my hearing and caused my ears to play tricks on me. I shook my head to clear it.

"What's that?" Vesper listened intently. Unless she suffered the same affliction as mine, the sound was not imaginary: bugles blowing the charge.

"The Legion!" cried Vesper.

The urgent, brassy notes grew louder. Within another moment, Colonel Marelle, saber out and flashing, galloped through the gates. Their cloth havelocks bright white in the sun, bayonets glinting, the Legionnaires streamed into Bel-Saaba. At the rear, mounted on a pair of racing camels, came Smiler and Slider.

"There!" Vesper pointed to the arcades. "Follow the Tawarik!"

Colonel Marelle, excellent officer that he was, understood the situation immediately.

"Mes enfants," he shouted, *"en avant!"*

With the banner of the Legion snapping in the breeze, his men raced after him, speeding to the relief of the embattled Beni-Brahim.

Without waiting for their camels to kneel, the twins jumped down and ran to Vesper. Their joy at our safety was cut short by the sight of An-Jalil.

Shouts of triumph rose from the direction of the town hall. The charge of bayonets in the hands of those grim-faced Legionnaires in the wake of the fierce Tawarik broke el-Khouf's men completely. Saving their own skins outweighed any loyalty to their vanished master. Flinging away their weapons, they took to their heels with such enthusiasm that even the Legion's famous quick pace could not overtake them.

"We did our best, Miss Vesper," Slider said. "Too late, it looks like."

"Seems that little shindy's over," Smiler added, in a tone of disappointment.

"Another's just starting," said Vesper, returning to An-Jalil. "We're going to win that one, too."

Vesper's optimism, I suspected, was more an attempt to raise her own spirits than a statement of fact. An-Jalil remained unconscious as his companions bore him through the jubilant crowd to the town hall and the chambers once occupied by el-Khouf.

Leaving his men in charge of his sergeant major, Colonel Marelle came to join us.

"I regret to see a gallant warrior in these painful circumstances," Marelle said. "As for you, Miss Holly, my men and I were glad for another opportunity to be of service. Thanks to Monsieur Sleedaire and Monsieur Smeelaire, who brought news of your captivity."

"Thanks more to Mr. Maleesh," put in Slider. "It was all his idea. We'd started thinking how to get Miss Vesper and the professor out of that library." He turned to Vesper. "After he went back and found you'd been taken off somewhere—unavailable for rescue, in a manner of speaking—he sent us to carry word to Mr. An-Jalil and borrow a pair of camels from him."

"Then he told us to ride hell-for-leather to Fort Iboush," said Smiler. "Which is what we did. You should have seen those Frenchies hustle. They got here in no time."

"It was Mr. Maleesh who told Doc Baba to set a smudge fire," added Slider. "If that sidewinder el-Khouf thought the old boy was in danger, he'd send his men to save him. Mr. Maleesh calculated how that would keep some of those guards too occupied to fight us."

"Maleesh planned the whole thing?" said Vesper. "What about the Beni-Brahim?"

"I don't rightly know," said Smiler. "That was Mr. Maleesh's own part in it. You'll have to ask him."

Though now apparent that Maleesh had masterminded a campaign that would have done credit to our gallant general and president, Ulysses Grant, he had not come to accept our grateful praise. He seemed, rather, to be making himself deliberately scarce.

Instead, it was Jenna who now hurried in with Dr. Baba.

"We came as soon as we learned what happened," said the aged scholar. "This young lady and I were tending the wounded. She has, by the way, proved to be a remarkable healer. Yes, yes, in time she could be a better one than I."

He and Jenna went quickly to examine An-Jalil. The old man turned away, shaking his head. "He may require more skill than the two of us possess."

Dr. Baba spoke hastily with Jenna, requesting her to fetch medicines. At his further instructions, Tashfin and Attia carried their unconscious leader into the adjoining chamber. Only Jenna, when she returned, was permitted to aid Dr. Baba. The grim Tawarik reluctantly waited in silence at the door. Vesper, despite her entreaties, was obliged to do likewise.

That night was as endless as any we had ever spent. From time to time, Jenna emerged to obtain materials from Dr. Baba's supply. When Vesper pressed her for word of An-Jalil, Jenna gave no answer.

In the course of our anxious waiting, Maleesh arrived with Sheik Addi. Seeing Vesper, Addi momentarily brightened, but he appeared in no mood for conversation.

Nor, for that matter, did Maleesh. When Vesper asked how he had managed to bring Sheik Addi and his band to our rescue, he was less than forthcoming.

"While the twin moons rode to Fort Iboush," he said tersely, "I set out to seek the Beni-Brahim. I found Sheik Addi almost at the city gates. I persuaded him to enter and help me find you."

"Then he's forgiven you!" exclaimed Vesper. "That's wonderful. Now, you and Jenna—"

Maleesh turned away, declining to say more.

Soon after dawn, Jenna and Dr. Baba stepped from the chamber. While Jenna ran to the arms of Maleesh, Dr. Baba approached us and the Tawarik.

"He will live." The old man smiled happily. "Yes, yes, he most assuredly will. Never have I seen one of such strength. Nor of such spirit.

"I feared I would be unable to treat his wound," he continued, "but I found the remedy. It was in the very book you returned to the library: Ibn-Sina's treatise on medicinal herbs. Without that, my child, your friend would not be alive at this moment—and asking to see you."

With a joyful cry, Vesper started up and would have gone into the chamber. Maleesh drew her back.

"Anisah," he said quietly, "now that all is well, I must take my leave of you. You asked why Sheik Addi agreed to help? He wished to regain his daughter, and I alone knew where to find her. I promised to bring Jenna to him.

"And one thing more," Maleesh added. "In exchange for his aid, I offered him my life as forfeit. Now I must pay with it."

144

❧ 24 ❧

Learning that one's beloved has bargained away his life must always come as a shock. Though Maleesh had made a sublimely heroic gesture, Jenna did not see it in that light. She beat her fists on his chest.

"Fool! Idiot! What have you done? You told me nothing of this. To make such a pledge with never a word, never a thought for me, for us!"

"I gave you all my thoughts," replied Maleesh. "I said nothing, for I knew you would try to keep me from it. Pearl of my heart, you have blessed me with more happiness than I dreamed would ever come to me. That, I owe to you. But I owe the *anisah* a different debt. In Mokarra, she saved my life. She gave me kindness when I most needed it. This weighs heavy in the scales of the universe."

"It doesn't weigh in Bel-Saaba," declared Vesper. "Maleesh, you don't owe me anything. In the Haggar, I set you free of your vow, didn't I?"

"So I thought," Maleesh answered. "Then I under-stood that freedom was not yours to give nor mine to accept. *Anisah,* I once told you that a golden chain linked our lives. It cannot be broken by words; it still binds me. So it is written."

"So it's also written," declared Vesper, "that you're not keeping that bargain."

"He will!" Sheik Addi burst out. "He pledged his life. It is mine to take. My hand shall strike him down!"

Jenna's eyes blazed as she flung herself in front of Maleesh. "You shall have to kill me first."

"Keep out of this!" roared Addi. "I decide who I kill and who I do not."

"No, you don't," retorted Vesper. "You won't lay a finger on either of them. You have no right. You aren't in your village; you're in Bel-Saaba. You've got no authority here. As long as Maleesh and Jenna are in the city, they're under the rule of the governor."

"El-Khouf has fled," Addi flung back. "There is no *kahia.*"

"That," said Vesper, "is what you think."

Leaving the Tawarik to keep Addi at bay, Vesper strode into the chamber. Held in Tashfin's grip, the sheik had to content himself with hurling insults at Maleesh, unrepeatable but not lethal.

After some while, Vesper put her head out of the door and beckoned to Dr. Baba. Puzzled, the old scholar went to join her. Vesper emerged again and invited all of us to enter.

With cushions under his head, An-Jalil lay on a divan. Without the covering of a veil or turban, his mane of hair hung about his brow and shoulders. His features, despite the blue stain, were pallid. Still, for one who had been shot at point-blank range, he looked in pretty fair condition.

"An-Jalil knows the bargain Maleesh made," said Vesper. "I was right. Addi has no authority over anybody in Bel-Saaba. That belongs to An-Jalil. He's the rightful governor and always has been."

"No, *anisah.*" An-Jalil raised a hand. "For your sake, I broke my vow. For your sake, I would break it again, a thousand times over. But, as I have told you, there is one oath I shall not break. I shall not accept to govern here."

"I understand that," said Vesper. "There was something else we talked about."

"As I also told you," said An-Jalil, "when there is no successor by birth, it is the right and duty of the governor to name who will take his place. This I now do.

"I choose one who is brave enough to admit his fear, and wise enough to admit that he is foolish; who would risk his life for one he loves, yet give up life and love if he believes he must. If he accepts, I name: Maleesh."

Maleesh stood too dumbstruck to answer.

Sheik Addi did it for him.

"He accepts!" Addi jubilantly roared. "And I accept him! My son-in-law—the *kahia*!"

He flung his arms around the joyous couple in such an embrace that Maleesh was in danger of being squashed before he could even start his administration.

Colonel Marelle, observing all this, now approached An-Jalil and saluted stiffly.

"An-Jalil es-Siba, it is my painful duty to place you under arrest."

CHAPTER

25

Colonel Marelle was either a man of incredible bravery or, what comes to much the same, a lunatic. Having made such an announcement, there was no way he would leave that room alive. Tashfin's dagger was already in his hand.

"Arrest me?" An-Jalil's eyes glinted. "Will you try your Legionnaires against my Tawarik?"

"I said it was my duty," replied Marelle. "I did not say I would carry it out. Why should I deprive myself of a gallant opponent? Another day, perhaps. Or perhaps not. Be warned. It may be different with those who someday will take my place. The times have changed. You, with your honor and chivalry, are not modern."

"Are you?" answered An-Jalil. "We are both only temporary. The desert and the mountains will outlive us. But a day must come when the French leave my land, as others before them have done."

"I do not speak as an officer of the Legion," said Marelle, "but as one who loves Jedera, and as one man to another. My friend, I hope you are right."

Dr. Baba, concerned that this was overtiring his patient, ushered all of us from the chamber and up to the balcony. At sight of their beloved benefactor, cheers burst from the waiting crowd below, and grew even louder when Dr. Baba presented Maleesh as the new governor.

"Maleesh is everything An-Jalil said he was," Vesper whispered to me. "Dr. Baba talked about frailties. Maleesh has enough of them, too, I daresay. He and Bel-Saaba are going to get along very nicely."

I agreed. After el-Khouf and so many other brutal governors, a fellow who could dance on his hands and pull coins from his nose would be a welcome change. It was fine for Bel-Saaba. It would, of course, never do for Philadelphia.

"An-Jalil made the perfect choice," Vesper added. "I'm glad I suggested it."

While An-Jalil continued to recover, Vesper and I at last had a chance to browse through the library. The workmen had, meantime, returned to the city. They reported that Helvitius had last been seen on a camel galloping across the desert.

"Too bad we didn't catch him," said Vesper. "Maybe he'll run into a sandstorm."

Though disappointed by the villain's escape, Vesper was more interested in the works of Ibn-Salah and reading his theories of flight for herself.

"Helvitius *did* misunderstand," she said, poring over the ancient volumes. "Yes—I can see how he miscalculated when he designed his flying machine. Ibn-Salah wasn't wrong; Helvitius was. Good thing these books are out of his reach. He won't come back to study them again. Besides, he's too arrogant to admit he made a mistake. He'll blame Ibn-Salah.

"Look here, Brinnie," she went on, "this diagram of how air flows over a curved surface—fascinating."

"Dear girl," I said, after urging Dr. Baba to lock up the precious volumes, "nature in her sublime wisdom has decreed that we shall not imitate the birds. A flying machine is impossible. As impossible as mankind ever setting foot on the moon."

"I wonder," said Vesper.

We remained in Bel-Saaba a few days more, until An-Jalil was well enough to leave the city. Colonel Marelle and his Legionnaires had already departed for Fort Iboush. Sheik Addi had grown even more overjoyed, envisioning his grandchildren and great-grandchildren, generation after generation of honored governors.

On our last morning, Jenna embraced us and the twins. *"Anisah,"* she said, "you have brought us life and happiness."

Maleesh echoed those sentiments and embraced us likewise, adding to Vesper, "Was I not right? The chain that links us is unbroken. So it is written, and so it is."

"Kahia Maleesh," replied Vesper, "you still have it backwards. First, it is. Then, so it will be written."

An-Jalil and his Tawarik escorted us back through the Haggar, this time following the longer but easier caravan trail. As a result, the journey was blessedly uneventful.

The Tawarik, however, would go no farther than Tizi Bekir.

"Here, *anisah,* we must part," said An-Jalil. "I long for my desert. I will be there as you voyage beyond the wide ocean." He touched his lips to his fingertips, which he gently pressed on Vesper's brow. "Salaam, *anisah.* Go in peace."

"And you," Vesper softly replied, returning his gesture. She smiled. "The spirit of the jinn flies where it wishes. Even to Philadelphia."

In Mokarra, we received unhappy news. The twins' ship had been burned past repair. There was no telling when Smiler and Slider could leave the country.

"We'll find another berth," said Smiler. "Don't worry. Slider and I can always manage."

"I'm sure you can," said Vesper. "But I've been thinking. You're clever with machinery. You could probably build a whole new sort of engine."

"No doubt of that," said Slider. "That's one of the things Smiler and I do best."

"Twins," said Vesper, "what would you think about coming to Philadelphia and staying with us?"

The offer of a trip to Philadelphia was one that could hardly be refused. Even so, Smiler and Slider glanced at each other uneasily.

"We'd be honored, Miss Vesper, as who wouldn't. But—we had that little misunderstanding with the law a few years back."

"No one's going to bother you now," said Vesper. "I'll see to it."

"Well, then," the twins replied simultaneously, "we couldn't ask better."

Fortunately, we had not long to wait for a vessel sailing to Philadelphia. The Tawarik had given us veils and tunics to replace our own garments and, for the sake of comfort, we wore them throughout the voyage. The veils especially offered excellent protection against wind and spray. However, the other passengers tended to give us a wide berth when they encountered us strolling the deck.

In Strafford, my dear Mary was delighted to make the acquaintance of Smiler and Slider, and welcomed them as happy additions to the household. She did show some dismay at our appearance.

"Poor child!" she exclaimed. "What's happened to you? And you, Brinnie! You've turned blue!"

"We'll explain later," said Vesper. "The main thing is, we returned the book."

"And quite properly so," said Mary. "You, my dear Brinnie, should feel especially edified at having done your duty."

"You'd have been proud of him," said Vesper. "If you'd seen him flying through the air—"

"What?" cried Mary. "Through the air? Brinnie!"

"He won't do it again," said Vesper, on her face a look of innocent sincerity which I knew all too well. "I promise he won't. Not for a while, anyhow."